ELISA ANN PRATT

Silver Linings: SECRETS

Book 2 of Silver Linings Trilogy

To my husband and children
To my Mom who always believed in my talent as a writer
To my inner child who truly needed this story to come out
To everyone who supported me in this process
#ShareTeam-You all know who you are!
Most of all for anyone else out there who feels alone, scared and will
hopefully be inspired by this story to find the light to the path of everything
they truly deserve. With Love and Light.
Note: This story is fictional, but the heartfelt emotions beneath its surface
are mine

Contents

Foreword

We were both trying to protect each other from our truths.

For my fellow music lovers out there, the following songs have all been a great inspiration to this story. I truly hope you enjoy the following playlist as much as I do.

I wanna know what love is - Foreigner
Iris - Goo Goo Dolls
Angel -Aerosmith
Sweetest Taboo - Sade
Nice and Slow - Usher
Hands to Heaven - Breathe
Piano in the Dark - Brenda Russell
Alone - Heart
I'll be there for you - Bon Jovi
Crazy for you - Madonna

Preface

This story contains sensitive material that may be disturbing to some readers for containing the following subjects: **abusive relationship, addiction, alcoholism, anxiety, sexual assault** and **sexually explicit content.** Reader discretion is advised.

Acknowledgement

Special thanks to L.B. Harpdog and C.H. Reece.
Both for taking valuable time out of their days to help me with my
tech challenges
Your help has made this process so much smoother and truly means
the world to me! Thank you both so very much!

Another Shout out to #ShareTeam -without your support, my book
baby would not have found it's way into the hands of my readers! I
love you all from the bottom of my heart!

And last, but most certainly not least, to my amazing ARC Team! I can
not wait to hear what you all think of this story! I just know you all
will help Silver Linings: Secrets find her success in the launch process
and I appreciate every single one of you! Thank you all so much! I
truly hope you all enjoy this story!

I

Part One

.

Chapter 1

A bigail Alexa Andrews came into this world a fighter. With nearly six hundred miles between us, I could only pray she would somehow draw from that strength to hold on. All I had to do was get to her before the demon that dwells inside AJ did.

It's crazy how a million thoughts can flutter through your mind a midst a wave of panic. How the finest of details strewn in from your bank of memories could splay across the screen of your mind, like clips from an old movie.

My baby sister, Abby, was born prematurely at eight months gestation from a high risk pregnancy. I may have been a little young at seven years old to have been thrown into the loop of things, however, concern was far too evident between Mama and Joel for it to remain hidden from me.

The tiny little pink jumper she wore was way too big for her premature size but I made Mama promise to dress her in it the day she came home from the NICU. I could almost hear the echoes of her little baby cries as I recalled how her hair smelled like baby powder when I held her in my lap for the very first time. She was mine. My baby sister.

Every night, I would lay on the floor next to her crib singing lullabies, reading stories and making promises. When Mama found me on the floor of her bedroom each morning with my blanket and pillow, eventually she accepted the fact that I refused to sleep in my own room anymore and convinced my step daddy, Joel, to move my bed into Abby's room, where it remained until she was a toddler. My biggest promise to Abby was that I would protect her always.

If I had known I would one day break those promises to keep her safe, I probably would never have voiced them. She was only an infant then, so of course she would never remember those promises. The truth was, I would and still did. And promises we make to others are promises we make to ourselves.

And now, knowing that everything could change in an instant was knowledge my heart just couldn't seem to bare. That a single omission to a story we tell in an attempt to protect someone we love could turn out to be the very thing that kills them. *God, please! If anything happens to her, I could never live with myself again. She has to be okay!* If I could only get there fast enough, maybe I won't be too late.

The traffic on the highway seemed to be moving at a good pace for a Monday. I breezed through several states as though they were nothing in the space of time in my mind that had been zipping through recollections of my past with Abby at the speed of light. When the indicator light went off in my car telling me I needed fuel, I stopped at the nearest gas station. If I could get to Virginia before nightfall, maybe it would be soon enough to avoid the potential reality my conscience

4

was purposely distracting me from.

I hung the nozzle back on its hook at the gas pump and quickly got back behind the wheel. I called Abby's phone what had to be over a hundred times, by now. Each and every time, my calls were sent straight to her voicemail. *That bastard probably turned the dang thing off!* I figured I would give it one more try before getting back on the highway. This time the phone was actually ringing... once, twice, three!

"I think he's dead..." Abby's voice muffled over the phone, followed by a continuous set of sobs.

"Abby, Oh my God. Abby, please, tell me that you're OK!" I was in shock as my mind began to process the fact that there was actually an answer on the call to fully comprehend what she was saying.

Incoherent cries continued. Clearly, Abby was not okay, but hearing her voice brought a total sense of relief to my entire being. If AJ was truly dead, he was no longer a threat to Abby. "Thank God you're okay, Abby! Where are you?"

Through her tears, she answered. "I'm still here. The police are here, Where are-" All I could make out was static on the line before it went dead.

"Abby... Abby? Yes, Abby! I'm coming, I'm coming!" I screamed into my dead phone, as if Abby could still hear me. *Damn it! Why of all times, did I not plug my damn phone in to charge last night? Because you were busy getting it on with Jasper, you fool!* My conscience was quick to reprimand me. *That's besides the point and truthfully had no bearings on the current situation at hand.* I quickly reminded myself.

I could feel the bile beginning to rise inside my stomach. I hadn't eaten a morsel all day. Hell, I barely even had anything to drink. My mind was steadily fixed on getting to Abby as quickly as possible.

Did she really just say that AJ was dead? I was more fixated on the fact that Abby was alive and hopefully out of danger to really process the message she delivered. At the very least, I knew she was alive and I knew where to find her. I was holding on to that for dear life!

I was beyond furious that AJ would even think about bringing Abby into this mess between us. He knew damn well just how much she meant to me. I was so mad, I could literally kill him myself. Figuratively though, not literally. I didn't really want him to die. If I was truly being honest with myself, somewhere in the depths of my heart, I still had love for AJ, despite all he had put me through.

~

AJ and I met at Wag's. It was a local diner, located in the center of town. I had just left a party with my friend Heather. AJ was there, sobering up after a night out drinking with his friends. With his mousy brown hair and big hazel green eyes, AJ boldly slid into my side of the booth and sold me a dream. I remember it, clear as day, his exact words. He was looking for a life partner. Someone to ride the storm with. What he saw in me that night, I'll never know.

I mean, it's not that I wasn't attractive. In fact, as I recalled, I was confidently dressed in my brand new clothes I recently bought to celebrate how hard I worked to lose those last few pounds. No, what baffled me lived somewhere within the contrast of how AJ treated me over the next two years. I could never seem to figure out why he chose me over all the other pretty girls in that crowded diner. I distinctly remember telling him that he would have to be the one to call me when we decided to exchange numbers because I knew I was too shy to make the first move.

Initially, I couldn't tell if I was even attracted to AJ, physically. He was a few years older than me and his build was slightly more stocky than I was used to with my former boyfriends. However, with a nudge from my friend Heather who was there the night we met, I caved and accepted a date with him when he called.

At the end of our first date, he invited me up to his apartment. At 21 years old, I was still naive to realize what that typically meant in the dating world. When his sexual advances toward me weren't reciprocated, he was quick to sense my unease and let go of his urges. That one single move was what hooked me. The fact that he intuitively respected the fact that I wasn't ready was something I could never attach to that evil force sucking every inch of life away from him now. A demon I had pronounced, the scapegoat, for all the damage he'd caused me. Unfortunately for me, that demon made his presence well-known a few short months after AJ and I started dating. Not soon enough, however, for my heart to fall in love with my rose-colored view of AJ and all the potential he had inside him.

AJ grew up on the other side of the tracks, you know, where doom and gloom lurked behind every shadow. Where children were often neglected and teenagers graduated childhood to the streets. It was no doubt, the link of our creativity was what strengthened our connection to one another.

I was born with an ability to see beyond the surface in people. A blessing and a curse. AJ captured my heart with his wounded soul and his undeniable potential. It was only in my nature to try and help him heal his inner child so he could see what he was truly capable of. Unfortunately, that awful demon had other plans.

Like me, AJ was a writer and also a musician. I could sit and listen to him play his guitar for hours. We even wrote a song or two together at one point. I often wondered why he couldn't just allow his creative works to fill his cup, rather than alcohol. If only he did, we would probably never be in this mess in the first place.

When things took a sudden turn south for us in Wakefield with AJ's new promotion, self sabotaging had taken over him to a point where AJ rarely spent any time on his talent anymore. In his downward spiral, AJ deteriorated himself and took me right along with him. With the absence of his creativity, eventually came my own. The storm had left us with no solid foundation to our relationship.

"Welcome to the State of Virginia" *Thank God!* I thought as I passed the sign on the highway. The sun was beginning to make its way toward the horizon, bringing a beautiful hue to the autumn colored leaves of the trees aligning the highway. If traffic continued its easy flow, I could surely make it there before dusk.

Chapter 2

I barely made my way onto the street of my old apartment. The parking lot was filled with an entire fleet of Wakefield police squad cars. Thankfully, I was able to find a spot to park in near the community pool a few blocks down.

Most would describe the tree-lined street I walked upon as beautiful as ever, dressed in the colors of fall, but to me, it was all a blur to my current reality. A sharp reality I would soon face.

My legs felt like jello when I finally reached the pathway to my old apartment with AJ. Suddenly, my need for hydration appeared to me in desperate measures. I had completely neglected my body's own basic needs just to get here as fast as I could.

There she was, leaned up against a squad car. She was wearing a white tee shirt and blue denim shorts. Her long, beautiful golden locks and warmly tanned skin glowed in the setting light of the sun. *Abby was alive!* It was hard to distinguish from my distant bloodshot view, but she appeared to be unscathed. *Thank you, God!*

"Carla!" She cried, looking over the shoulder of the female detective who stood in front of her holding a notepad.

"Abby! I'm here!" I cried back as I made an attempt to run towards her. All of a sudden, my legs buckled beneath me.

~

I woke up in a hospital bed, attached to an IV that was feeding me fluids. Abby sat in the chair next to my bed, resting her head beside me with her hand cradled over mine. Poor thing must have been exhausted after everything she'd gone through. She had fallen asleep and since I was still tired and didn't want to wake her, I let my head fall back against the pillow. I closed my eyes and fell back asleep, myself.

An hour or so later, I was stirred awake by a gentle caress to my forehead. I opened my eyes to a face I would easily recognize from anywhere. An older version of myself, complete with long wavy auburn hair to match. For a moment, it hit me just how long it had been since I had last seen her.

"Mama..." I said with a swipe of my hand to brush away a single tear from my eye.

"Yes, baby. It's me. I'm here." She said. A small smile spread across her fair complexion. Her expression told me that whatever I was in here for, I was going to be okay.

"Oh, Mama, I'm so sorry." I said, tears rolling down my face as everything began to resurface in my mind.

"It's okay, honey." She consoled me.

"Where's Abby? Is she okay?" I asked, my voice laced with concern.

"She's gonna be okay. She's shaken up, but she's more worried about you than she is of herself."

"Are you sure? I was so worried, Mama!" I asked, recalling the images I had envisioned of her being tied up and at the mercy of AJ's evil demon.

"Yes, Baby. She's fine. She'll be right back, she went to get us some coffee. How are *you* feeling?" She asked, bringing my attention to the fact that it was *me* who *was* currently lying in a hospital bed.

"I feel fine." I said. "I'm more worried than anything else. I'll feel better once I see Abby."

A knock on the door alerted us before it opened, softly. A nurse walked in through the door. She was there to take my vitals.

"Glad to see you're awake. Everything looks good. Doc says you're good to go as soon as we draw up your paperwork. You'll just have to take it easy and make sure to keep yourself hydrated from now on." She said, before leaving the room.

"You're awake!" Abby cried, barging passed the nurse on her way in through the door. She set the tray of coffee onto a small side table in the corner of the room and came around to the other side of the bed to hug me. "Thank God! I was so worried!"

"*You* were worried? I was worried about *you!* I'm so sorry, Abby. I had no idea he would bring you into this mess between us!" My eyes were filled with tears. I couldn't help thinking that if I had just told her the truth, this could have all been avoided. "My God, if anything were to happen to you-" I said, my voice trailing off with my imagination.

A knock at the door interrupted our conversation. The person behind it made my jaw drop to the floor. *This can't be happening? I must be dreaming.* Still as reality would have it, in walks Jasper, all 6 feet of brown hair, blue eyed gorgeousness that he was made of.

"They told me I could find you here. Are you alright?" He asked. "I hope you don't mind, I had to tell them I was your brother." Instinctively, I gathered the blanket in my fists to pull it up over my body to cover myself. Surely, I was a disgraceful mess and in no way, shape or form ready for the mercy of those angelic eyes of his.

"Oops! I didn't have a chance to tell you about the hot guy who was looking for you out in the hallway." Abby chimed in with a cute little smirk spread across her face. *Uh, yeah! That piece of information definitely would have been nice to know before he came in here.* I let Abby off the hook since she really didn't have time to tell me.

"Jasper!" I shouted out in surprise. "What are you doing here?"

"'I'll have to explain that later, I'm just glad to see you're alright." He said, extending his hand out to Mama. "Hi, I'm Jasper, by the way. I'm..." he stopped to exchange glances with me. "I'm a friend of your daughter's." He was clearly trying to gauge the situation without giving away too much information.

12

"Hi, Jasper, I'm Corrine. Carla's mother." Mama said, warmly. "And this here is Abby, Carla's sister." Mama continued, placing her hands on each of Abby's shoulders. "I'm afraid Carla hasn't mentioned you before." Confusion flashed in the crease of Mama's eyebrows as she turned to face Abby. "Abby, why don't we go find some snacks and let these two have a moment to talk."

"But I just-" Abby bit out before Mama nudged her out of the room. Abby was obviously curious about Jasper and me. And in this moment, so was I!

"I don't understand… How did you even know where to find me?" I asked.

"When I came home, I noticed you left without your sweater and never touched the croissants I brought for you. It didn't sit right with me, but I let it go." Jasper started as he took a seat in the chair next to my bed and placed his hand in my lap. "When you didn't show up for work or return my calls or text messages, I was really beginning to worry. Then Charlie, the security guard, told me you left in a hurry as if something was wrong. It was then that I met your friend Jamie out in the lobby. She asked me if I knew where you were because she hadn't heard from you either. When she told me your mother couldn't get a hold of you and that your sister went missing, I hopped on the next flight I could find."

"I see. So you came all the way to Virginia to *rescue* me?" I asked, still trying to wrap my head around everything.

"I swear, I'm not a stalker!" Jasper laughed realizing how it must have appeared, him showing up out of nowhere. "Forgive me, but with everything you told me, I didn't trust your asshole ex-boyfriend. I just came to make sure you were safe and help you find your sister."

"Thank God she's okay." I said as the tears began to pool inside my eyes, again.

Jasper stood up. He offered me the box of tissues that were sitting next to the sink behind the bed and sat back down in the chair next to me. "Yes, it looks like she's gonna be fine. I overheard the nurses talking. I think your ex is here in another room somewhere."

"Hold on, are you saying that AJ's still alive?" I asked. "Abby said she thought he was dead."

"I don't know much, just the few things I overheard in the hallway. He came in with alcohol poisoning, but I think he might pull through."

The nurse knocked softly on the door and entered the room again. This time, she had my release paperwork in her hands. "Okay, I'll just need you to sign a few things and you're good to go." She handed me a clipboard of documents and a pen.

"I'm going to step out for a moment to see if I can find your mother and sister to let them know they're ready to let you out of here, I'll be right back." Jasper said, before leaving the room.

Chapter 3

After signing all the paperwork, I stepped out into the hallway to see if I could find Mama and Abby. When I passed by AJ's room, I paused to look inside. The curtains were drawn open and I was able to get a look at him. He was sleeping. He looked so lifeless. My mixed emotions were all so consuming. I was incredibly angry, sad and admittedly worried all at the same time. I stood there, frozen in silence, contemplating on whether to open the door to see him when Mama came up behind me. She gently draped her arm around my shoulder and pulled me away from the door.

"Trust me, honey. You're better off leaving him alone," She said as she guided me toward the front entrance of the hospital.

Jasper was pulled up along the curb, outside waiting for me. He got out of the SUV and opened the passenger door the moment he saw me step outside. He took my hand and lead me to the passenger seat of his rental car. Abby was parked right behind him in Mama's car.

"Your mom and Abby are going to follow us to the Waffle Iron next to the hotel we're staying at. I booked an extra room for the night so they won't have to drive back home so late," Jasper said.

"You didn't have to do that-" I started to say.

"Please don't be upset, it's the least I could do after everything they've been through," Jasper said, reassuringly.

"I'm not upset. What I meant was that you have already come so far just to see if I was alright. Of course, I don't want them to drive home after everything either. Honestly, I really appreciate the gesture," I breathed. I didn't want to seem like I was being rude.

"Don't worry, I already told you I can easily afford it and I'm happy to. I'm also glad, because it's already been settled," He said with a chuckle. "Apparently your mom and sister were far easier to convince.

"So they already know about the room?" I asked.

"Yes, your mother was worried about the dog, but she agreed anyway as long as she could leave early in the morning." Jasper replied.

"Oh shoot, that's right! What about Lucas?" I asked, curiously.

"He's fine. Tony's looking after him while I'm gone," Jasper replied. "I'm sure his wife will be sending *him* to the doghouse after this," he laughed, "but I wouldn't take no for an answer. And I think we both know I can be pretty persuasive when I want to be." Jasper replied, coolly.

The all forgotten butterflies made their debut to the pit of my stomach

16

as I let my mind wander down the gutter at the mere mention of his words. *Persuasive was an understatement!*

The orange neon sign for Waffle Iron appeared as we turned the corner. Through the rear view mirror, I could see Mama and Abby following us into the parking lot. *This ought to be interesting!* I thought to myself as we all got out to make our way inside the diner.

~

"Have you ever been to a Waffle Iron before?" I asked Jasper as the four of us crammed into the tiny little booth that was barely big enough for us all to sit together. It was almost midnight and the diner was practically empty.

"No, I'm afraid this is my first time," Jasper laughed as he glanced down at the menu, while picking his arm up from the table so the busboy could wipe it down. The towel was doused in a mixture of bleach and water. I got a whiff and my insides began to churn at the scent. The smell of bleach had always made me feel nauseous.

"I'll have a decaf coffee with milk and Splenda on the side, please." I said to the curvy blonde waitress, who quickly appeared to take our order.

"Just a plain waffle and black coffee, please," Mama said as she handed the waitress her menu.

"Pecan waffle with chocolate chips and Marshmallow sauce for me!" Abby said. "Ooh, and a chocolate milk, please!"

"That sounds good," Jasper said with a wink to Abby as he gave the waitress his menu. "I'll have what she's having. Just plain milk for me, please."

"Well… This is cozy." Mama said, smiling. "Thank you again, for getting us a room for the night, that was very thoughtful of you," Mama said to Jasper.

"It's no trouble at all. I'm happy you agreed to stay. I think we could all use a good night's sleep after all this, anyway," Jasper said to Mama.

"Clearly we have a lot to talk about, here. So why don't we start with how you two know each other." Mama asked me.

After a quick glance over at Jasper, I let him take the lead.

"Well, it's actually a funny story. I don't really think Carla knows this, but the first time I saw your daughter was at the Grand Opening of my night club in Boston," Jasper said with his eyes on me. The look of surprise on my face matched both Mama and Abby's as we all locked in on him to proceed.

"There was something about her that struck me. Quite honestly, I couldn't seem to get her angel face off my mind," Jasper laughed. "So when Lucas, had the audacity to steal her lunch at the park, a few days later, I just knew we were destined to meet."

"Wait! Who's Lucas and why would he steal Carla's lunch?" Abby asked.

Jasper replied with a chuckle. "Lucas is my dog."

I sat there in shock for a moment. I had no idea he saw me at the club that night. "Hold on a minute. You own Club Hush?"

"It's one of the investments I mentioned to you. My friend Sam needed some financial backing, so technically, I own half of the club."

"I had no idea!" I said with a look of shock spread across my face. "When did you see me?" I dared myself to ask as I recalled my awful panic attack from that night.

"I saw you dancing with your friend, Jamie. You seemed a bit out of sorts. I thought you were strikingly beautiful, unlike anyone else I had ever seen before. I was going to introduce myself and bring you off the dance floor for a drink, but then I lost sight of you in the crowd," Jasper replied. "A few minutes later, I saw you run past me, crying. I felt awful and wanted to see if you were alright, but I lost track of where you went." Jasper said, describing my panic attack at the club from an outside perspective to a tee. I was stunned by Jasper's revelation. It all made perfect sense now. It was why he seemed so familiar to me when we first met that day at the park.

"I didn't know." I said. "I was so embarrassed that night because it was the first time Jamie and I had ever gone out with her friends."

"Oh, honey… why didn't you tell me you were having such a hard time? That must have been awful for you." Mama said to me as she placed her hand over mine from across the table and gave it a squeeze.

"It's just embarrassing, Mama. You know how much I hate crying in front of people. I'm fine now, truly." I replied, withdrawing my hand from Mama's to swipe my bangs behind my ears like a curtain. A tell tale sign that I was nervous. "What I would really like to know is how you wound up with AJ in my old apartment?" I asked as I placed my full attention on Abby. Jasper pulled me in closer to his side and I couldn't help but notice how my tension melted away like magic The effect this had on me was nothing short of miraculous.

"I was walking home from school when AJ offered me a ride. I didn't think anything of it and it was so hot outside. He said he needed my help, that you were coming home, and that he wanted to surprise you for your birthday. He promised to have me back home before my curfew if I came over to help him decorate your apartment." Abby said as the waitress came to the table with our drinks.

"I was excited to see you, so of course, I agreed." Abby continued. "We went to the dollar store and bought a bunch of balloons, party streamers, and even a box of cake mix. When we got into town, he stopped in at the corner store and picked up a twelve pack of beer and something else in a brown bag. I just assumed it was your birthday gift. I didn't know he was a drunk, Carla!" Abby cried to me in an apologetic tone. "I found out as the day went on. He kept saying you were on your way... but I knew something wasn't right, the more he drank. So when it started to get late, I told him I was going to call Mama to pick me up because he was too drunk to drive." Abby cocked her head to the side to face Mama. "That's when he grabbed my phone away from me. He showed me his gun and made me sit on the couch." Abby paused to take a gulp of chocolate milk through her straw. "He never touched me, Carla. I hope you believe me. He just kept saying over and over that I wasn't what he wanted. He was so angry with me because I wasn't you. He refused to let me get off the couch... only once to use the bathroom. And even then, he stood right outside the door and made me keep it open. All night, he went on and on about how you ruined his life. That everything was fine until you made him move away. I was so scared, Carla. More for you than me because I thought you were coming home to him." Hearing Abby's words cut deep. Although I was relieved to hear that AJ didn't physically touch Abby, I could still feel my knuckles turning white as my hands clenched into fists beneath the table. The thought of her being afraid for my life and not knowing what might possibly happen to her, all because I decided to keep the truth from her was really eating me up. I was so angry with AJ. I couldn't even formulate a response. *Why did he have to bring her into this?*

"My Goodness! What a nightmare?! That must have been awful for you, baby." Mama said, drawing Abby in a nurturing embrace. "I had no idea AJ was even capable of kidnapping. That certainly wasn't the young man I met. Thank God things didn't escalate any further than they did," Mama said as she fixed her gaze on me. "You said you two weren't getting along, but you never told me he was an alcoholic, Carla. You know I fought so hard to keep you far away from that with your father when you were little. Why didn't you tell me what was going on?" Mama asked, piercing a dagger straight into my already wounded heart. Tears began to erupt down my face, illuminating the redness in my cheeks that were already hot from anger. My emotions were all over the place.

"Forgive me," Coming to my defense, Jasper quickly interjected as he found my hand under the table to give it a squeeze. "I think we should give Carla a break and be thankful that everyone is going to be okay. This has all been torturous enough for everyone. I'm sure Carla had her reasons to keep her private business to herself."

"I didn't come to you because I knew you would be upset with me. I knew you wouldn't understand why I had chosen to stay with AJ. You always said I was better off without my father, Mama, but it never changed the fact that I still missed him every day. I just thought that maybe I could choose a different path than you did with my father. Perhaps there might be a better outcome for AJ. Like somehow, if AJ could get better, then maybe it was possible for my own father to get better. I didn't know things would get as bad as they did. I never imagined he would do something like this, Mama. You have to believe me." I said through my tears as the waitress awkwardly approached our table, interrupting the conversation with our food. The air fell silent.

"Well, I don't know about you guys, but I'm starving!" Abby said, breaking the silence as she reached for her fork. "And personally, I'm just happy to have this opportunity to finally see my big sis and her new.... friend." She added with a smile while stabbing the waffle she had drenched in marshmallow sauce with her fork and knife.

"I suppose you're right, it's all water under the bridge," Mama concluded. "I am happy you two are safe now. And it is nice to see you Carla, and to have the chance to meet you, Jasper."

"This looks fantastic, Abby. Great choice!" Jasper chimed in to agree as he took a bite of his own waffle. Watching everyone else try to let things go brought me some relief. Enough to at least pretend like my appetite was present enough for me to eat. I took a few bites for show and asked the waitress to box up the rest. My stomach was still in knots.

22

Chapter 4

⌁

After checking in at the hotel, Jasper and I walked Mama and Abby to their room just down the hall from ours. It was difficult not to take notice at how much fancier this place was than the motel I had stayed at on my way up to Boston. Everything was crisp and clean and literally smelled luxurious. There were beautiful paintings aligning the walls. Dark red, and vibrant yellow geometric shapes were splattered across the well padded navy blue carpeting beneath our feet as we made our way down the hall.

"Don't forget, we have to be up early tomorrow. I told Detective Stacy we would be there before noon for questioning," Abby said to me as we approached the door to their hotel room. This was news to me. I imagined the appointment must have been arranged while I was sleeping.

The idea of being questioned by a detective about my relationship with AJ seemed as enticing as being kicked in the gut! After seeing him lying there in that hospital bed, looking so defenseless, I was completely torn between seeking justice and extending grace.

If there was one thing I knew for certain, I was far from ready to deal with what was to come. In fact, I'd have been perfectly content with shoving it all in the past and never looking back if only it were an option. With law enforcement stepping in now, I had no choice but to suck it up and press through.

"I'm afraid I will have to leave early in the morning. I have a client and Crystal needs to go out before I go to work. I was hoping you guys could bring Abby home afterwards. Can you do that for me?" Mama asked. "I hate that I won't be there with you girls." She added with a sigh.

"Of course... Don't you worry about that. We'll make sure she gets home." I said to Mama. I was certainly up for the task of anything I could do to begin to redeem myself.

"Thank you," Mama said. "Please call me afterwards to let me know how everything goes."

"Okay, we will. I love you Mama. I'm so sorry about all of this," I said. I gave her and Abby a hug.

"Give us a call when you wake up in the morning and we'll go have breakfast before we go down to the station," Jasper said to Abby.

"I will." Abby said, blushing from the attention she was given.

"It was so nice to meet you Corrine, please try to get a good night's sleep and have a safe trip home," Jasper said to Mama.

"The pleasure was all mine, honey." Mama said, sighing. "I just wish the circumstances were better."

"They will be next time," Jasper said, comfortingly. "Good night, ladies."

"Good night!" Abby called out from the bed she let herself collapse into before Mama closed the door behind them.

Chapter 5

Our room was just a few doors down the hall from Mama and Abby's. I was far from looking forward to what was to come the following day. All I wanted was to get a shower and just relax. It had been a long day between the drive down and being in the hospital and just everything. My emotions had my nerves all over the place. *Why can't I just let things go?* I felt so guilty for not being more open with Mama and Abby about what I had been dealing with all these months. If only I had, perhaps everything could have easily been avoided.

It was quite a surprise, having Jasper show up. I never would have dreamed in a million years that he would. After all, we had only just met. It made me wonder if his initial attraction to me somehow matched my own for him. *Did he feel the magic too?*

"Which side of the bed do you prefer?" Jasper asked me, jolting me out of my deep seated thoughts as we walked through the door of our hotel room.

Again, it was hard not to differentiate between this place and the Highway Lodge Express. The mini bar welcomed our entry with its various offerings of keurig style coffees and teas. An aroma of freshly baked chocolate chip cookies alerted me to a basket full of them sitting on the counter top. Below the bar, there was a fully stocked fridge with a wide array of mini bottles of wine and all sorts of liquor.

"That is if you don't mind sharing the bed with me," he said with that famous sexy smirk of his. "I could exchange for a double bed room if you need me to." *As if!* Sharing a bed with Jasper was the one thing I was *really* looking forward to throughout this whole ordeal.

"Hmm… I'll take the left side, thanks," I hummed my reply. "If you don't mind, I could really use a hot shower. That hospital bedding was starting to make my skin feel itchy."

"Not at all. Make yourself at home. I was going to call Tony anyway to see how Lucas is doing. Everything you need should be up there," Jasper replied, pointing to the double vanity area adjoining the bathroom. It was neatly stocked with various sizes of towels, some were even folded into cute little animal shapes. There were fancy soaps and any other toiletry product one could ever possibly need. They even offered plastic wrapped toothbrushes for guests who may have forgotten to bring their own.

Inside the bathroom, lay a Jacuzzi-style tub and a separate stall for showering. If I weren't exhausted, I would have loved to have taken full advantage of the tub. Since Jasper came all the way here to *rescue* me, I didn't want to be rude. I opted for a quick shower instead.

The water felt satisfying and warm against my skin. I almost didn't want to get out, but I knew Jasper was just beyond that bathroom door and I didn't want to keep him waiting too long. I had to take a minute to fully appreciate the fact that he had really come through for us today. He was my very own silver lining in this entire shit storm of chaos that had been surrounding me. In that moment, I honestly felt like the luckiest girl alive to have found him.

When I stepped out of the shower dressed only in the luxuriously, soft white cotton bathrobe that had been so graciously provided by the hotel, I realized I didn't have any clean clothes to change into. I was also surprised to find the room empty when I came out of the bathroom. *Where did he go?* I checked to see if he may have stepped out onto the balcony, but he was nowhere to be found. For a moment, my heart began to sink. *He wouldn't come all the way down here just to abandon me, would he? I'm sure he'll be back soon.* I told myself to move on from my doubt.

I needed to call Jamie to let her know I was okay but I didn't have my charger and my battery was still dead on my phone. After being gone for so long, I just knew she would be worried sick! Perhaps I could call Mama or Abby and ask them to send her a text message for me. I wanted to at least let her know I was alive so she wouldn't have to worry.

Just as I picked up the phone to dial the extension to their room, I heard the click of the hotel room door indicating that the key card was placed inside the scanner. Jasper casually walked inside holding a large gift bag with a giant teddy bear peeking out from the top and a birthday balloon. I was shocked to see that he actually remembered. Frankly, with everything going on, I had completely forgotten it was my birthday. My face lit up in surprise. I quickly hung the phone back on the receiver.

"Damn it! I wanted to surprise you... I was hoping to get back before you came out of the shower" He laughed. "Happy Birthday, Angel!" he said as he stalked his way over to kiss me on the forehead.

"I honestly forgot it was my birthday... you really didn't have to go all out!" I cried as Jasper handed me the bag with my gift. Underneath the teddy bear, there was a soft white t-shirt with "Virginia" written across it and a plain white box that was tied with a string.

"As gorgeous as you are in that bathrobe I sure wouldn't mind untying you from, I figured you might want something a little more comfortable to sleep in. Unfortunately, they didn't have much of a selection in the gift shop." He said. "Go ahead... open the box."

"That was still very thoughtful of you, thank you." I said, feeling feverish. His sensual choice of wording created quite an image in my mind.

As he commanded, I carefully untied the string to the box. Inside, there were two vanilla bean cupcakes that were iced in a decadent buttercream and topped with 2 fresh raspberries that were nestled inside a bed of raspberry jam. The aroma quickly assaulted my senses and made my mouth begin to water the moment I peeked inside the box.

"I hope you like raspberries... Unfortunately, they were all out of candles, so I'll have to improvise. The lady at the gift shop said her sister runs a small bakery from home and she brings them in fresh daily. She also said I would thank her later if I bought one." Jasper came up behind me to get a whiff of the contents inside the box from over my shoulder. "You know, I couldn't resist buying one for my angel on her birthday." *His Angel?!* I swear, this guy had all the right things to say to make my imagination run wild.

Jasper quickly drew a lighter from the pocket of his jeans and flicked the flame as he serenaded me with the 'happy birthday' song. I swear, it was the sweetest thing ever! *"M*ake a wish!" He said. I closed my eyes, made a wish and blew out the flame.

"My wish is already here." I said, staring up at him with hungry eyes. Jasper, a quick study, took the box of cupcakes out of my hand and set it on top of the nightstand next to the bed. He walked over to the edge where I was sitting and slowly began to remove his gray and white flannel shirt as I silently thanked the heavens for whoever invented the button. The slow burn of desire rose to the brim of my fingertips, enchanting them with the power to draw his t-shirt off his body, myself. Surprised by my own courage, a giggle quickly escaped my throat. Jasper quickly found my lips to silence my laughter. Our tongues crash into one another. Suddenly, I was reminded of my duty to call Jamie. It just wouldn't be right to let her continue through the night worrying about me.

"Wait… I forgot, I really need to call Jamie," I said, reluctantly pulling myself away from the trance I was in.

"Don't worry, your mom already spoke to her, she called while they were releasing you from the hospital," He said breathing heavily. He quickly drew me back to the passion between us with a single flash of his eager blue eyes. He stood there before me, seeking my eyes with his own. I was baffled by his ability to keep the fire burning while maintaining his stance of being a gentleman.

Like a moth to a flame, I could never resist those eyes of his. I confirmed my willingness with a nod and nearly lost it when he licked his lips and untied my robe to reveal my naked body beneath it. He moved in closer between my knees when I scooted myself back on the bed to give him the space he needed to climb on top of me.

"If I could kiss away every inch of you that asshole ever laid his hands on, I would. You're mine now, you hear me?" He whispered to my ear before nipping at my earlobe. The sensation sent shivers all the way down my spine.

"I hear you, Jasper. Yours and only yours." I said in response as he continued to kiss his way down the side of my neck and back up to my lips. My heart was pounding so fast, I could feel it vibrating between us. This was nothing like I had ever experienced before. Hearing Jasper stake his claim on me, while displaying his affection really did a number on my emotions. It was like the stress of the whole day hit me all at once and melted away at his touch. From that point, there was nothing I could do to stop my tears from falling.

"Please don't cry, Angel." He said, cupping my face to wipe my tears away with the pad of his thumb. "As bad as I want you right now, it is getting late. I think maybe we should try to get some rest. You've been through a lot today and tomorrow is a big day." He planted a soft kiss in the space between my eyebrows and gently tugged me into his arms.

"I suppose you're right." I agreed. "I'm really not looking forward to tomorrow. I wish I could just leave it all in the past."

"You're so strong, I have no doubt you'll be able to handle it. I'll be here and so will Abby. I promise you, whatever tomorrow brings, we will face it together. You have my word," He said.

"I really appreciate you for saying that. I feel so much better knowing that you're here with me." I said, shifting over to my side so my back was pressed against his chest. What I needed to say next would be easier if I weren't face to face with him. "I just don't know if I'm ready to open up about everything. I don't even like thinking about it because I really did love AJ. I know deep down, he's a good person, but the things that would come up would definitely have him arrested."

"Listen Baby," he said, wrapping his arms around me, "If there is anything I have learned in life, it's this. We must take ownership of our shit. I wasn't always a saint. I've done things I'm not proud of, but I had to take a good hard look in the mirror before I could accept it. Before any change can happen, we really have to be willing to deal with whatever it was that brought us to darkness in the first place. Along with that will come acceptance of the fact that we often tend to hurt people we care about in the process. It's a process most are not willing to approach, because the battle is long and hard and oftentimes we have to do it all on our own." I couldn't imagine what darkness may have ever been lurking inside Jasper. He did suffer quite a bit of tragedy as a child, so I certainly understood that it may have taken him some time to recover from it.

"I know it sucks having to be the one to drive that nail in AJ's coffin. Especially after having dealt with all the garbage he's put you through. Without accountability, AJ may move on to someone else and continue the cycle. I know you well enough to know that if you could stand up for that next girl, you absolutely would." *Seriously? Where did this guy come from? And how on earth did I get so lucky to find him?* I wondered. The way he put things gave me the perspective I needed. I now knew exactly what I needed to do, but it was going to take a world of courage on my part.

"I guess I never thought of it that way before. You're so right." I said, sighing. It still didn't make things easy, but I knew I had to do what was right. I couldn't live with myself knowing that some other girl might end up in the same position I was in or worse.

"One way or another, we will get through it, Angel. I promise, you will never be alone in this." Jasper said, strengthening his grasp around me. "Let's get some rest." With the comfort of his words and the warmth of his body wrapped around me, my nerves finally settled and we both fell asleep.

Chapter 6

AJ

"I already told you, ma'am... I picked her up to help me plan a surprise birthday party for my girlfriend, what more do you want from me?" I said to the officer staring back at me. Her narrowed amber brown eyes continued to drill me as if they were expecting my story to change. "Now will you please tell me why I'm handcuffed to this bed?"

"So you didn't force Abby to stay at your apartment against her will?" Detective Stacy asked as she scribbled something down in her notepad. *What the hell is she writing?*

"Nah, man... She wanted to help me. It's her sister. Why is that so hard for you to understand? I never would've picked her up in the first place if she didn't want to come help me."

"I see... And you have nothing further to add to your statement?" She asked as she fastened the top to her pen and hooked it back into her breast pocket.

"Statement for what? No! Now can you please tell me what the hell is going on?" I could barely remember coming home in the first place, I damn sure didn't have the answers she was looking for.

"You were brought in here last night because you nearly drank yourself to death. You were passed out with a blood alcohol level of 0.25 when we responded to the call. What about the gun? Where did you put the gun?"

"Gun? What gun? What are you talking about?" *Fuck if I knew!* The only gun I owned was the pistol my grandpa gave me before he died. I didn't even have any bullets for it. Hell, I'd be surprised if it still worked in the first place. "Did someone get shot or something? Why won't you tell me what the fuck is going on?"

"No one got shot. I have what I need for now. I'll be back later once you've calmed down a bit. Get some rest before you get yourself in any more trouble." Detective Stacy said before she turned on her heels and headed out the door of the hospital room I was detained in.

Jasper

After overhearing the exchange of words between the detective and AJ, I watched as the detective left AJ's room. Now was my only chance to do what I came to do. A quick glance at my watch told me I had to work fast if I wanted to get back to the hotel before Carla woke up.

As much as it pained me to try and help this asshole, I knew it was important to Carla. She had already suffered enough. It killed me listening to her cry while she slept, last night. The last thing she needed right now was having to relive everything she tried to escape. If I can somehow get my plan to work, maybe AJ could be saved. One thing I knew for sure, he would never come near her again. Not after I was done with him.

The officer guarding AJ's room was preoccupied, watching the news on the TV. I sneaked past him and crept into AJ's room.

"Who the fuck are you?" AJ was quick to ask when he saw me.

"First off, you better watch your tone with me. And keep your voice down," I said, pointing to the guard who was stationed just outside AJ's room. "I'm the guy who's gonna try to save your ass from some of the shit you dug your way into."

"What the fuck are you talking about? I don't even know who you are, man! Or why I'm handcuffed to this bed in the first place," AJ said, lowering his voice.

"Make no mistake, I'm the same asshole you'll never want to meet again. I swear to God, if you ever come near Carla or Abby or anyone she cares about again, I will end you, do you hear me?" I said in an authoritative tone.

"Carla's *my* fucking girlfriend, asshole-" AJ bit out. I quickly placed my hand over his mouth.

"I said, watch your tone! You're here because you kidnapped her baby sister and kept her all through the night until they found your sorry ass passed out on the living room floor. I'm going to say it one more time so you understand me. I am going to try to help you get out of some of the trouble you're in, but so help me God, if you dare come near Carla, her family or anyone she's close to again, we will meet again. And next time, I won't be so fucking understanding. You got me?" AJ wiggled his head beneath the grasp of my hand.

"Consider yourself lucky that Carla thinks you're worth saving. You're gonna have to help yourself to do it, so suck it up! If you think you're big and bad now, putting your hands on a lady, you just wait and see how tough you are in prison." AJ huffed and puffed through my fingers until he relaxed his eyebrows, finally admitting defeat. I removed my hands from over his mouth.

"I don't remember any of that." AJ said. The frustration in his voice sounded genuine.

"Listen, all you have to do is be honest about everything. From whatever it is that you actually can remember and I will try to work everything else out. If I'm lucky enough to get them to listen to me, they will send you to rehab "

"I'm not rich, man. I can't afford to go to *rehab!*" AJ protested.

"Don't worry about that, I'll handle it." I said. AJ turned away from me and looked out the window, but said nothing.

"Look, I'm sure there's some sob story that brought you to where you are now, but you better figure it the fuck out! And keep your sorry-ass, cowardly hands off the ladies from now on. You're bigger than that, bro. At least Carla thinks so and I hope I am right by putting my trust in her instincts. This is your one and only get out of jail free card, motherfucker so you better take it. Understand?! If you don't, I will personally see to it myself that Carla presses charges against everything you did to her. She's mine now… Don't think for a second I won't kill you myself with my bare hands if you ever come near her again." The expression on AJ's face told me he was smart enough to know I had him by the balls.

"Whatever dude." AJ said. It was enough for me to trust that he knew I meant every word I said to him. I quickly slipped out of the room without the guard noticing and made my way back to the hotel.

Chapter 7

Carla

I was awakened by the touch of Jasper's hands at my feet. He smoothed through each and every little toe with the tips of his fingers and worked his palms to the base of my foot to massage each and every tendon, releasing its tension. *This was nice!* I kept my eyes closed as his fingertips slowly trickled upwards to skate along the muscles of my calves. He stopped to gently caress behind my knees, making my entire body tingle from the inside out. I grabbed the pillow from his side of the bed and pulled it over my face to stifle an inescapable moan.

"Good morning, Angel." He whispered. The guttural tone in his voice instantly beckoned the butterflies from deep within the core of my belly.

"Good morning." I said through the pillow, my voice was still embarrassingly hoarse from sleeping.

"I worked some things out to make today a little easier for you," he said. "But first, I'm going to make you feel so relaxed, it won't even feel like any of that even matters." I cleared my throat and tossed the pillow from over my head aside.

I forced myself to peek my head out from underneath the pillow. "Is that so?" I asked, my interest was piqued.

"It's a fact. Now lay back and let me take care of you." He demanded.

Far from protesting his command, I did as he said. I was taken by surprise when he shifted his pace, swiftly hooking his hands beneath my thighs to pull my entire body closer to the edge of the bed until he was satisfied with my positioning. I watched him in wonder as he bowed down on the floor to his knees and slowly planted feather soft kisses up my inner thighs until he reached the rim of my silky, soft panties. He wasted no time in sliding them off with his strong, calloused hands and quickly nuzzled his mouth into my softened lips.

My body was still fixed in a state of relaxation from my recent slumber. Every sensation was intensified, tenfold. The butterflies were thrilled to fasten their seat belts for the roller coaster ride of their life. I gasped the second he put his mouth on me and quickly bit down on my finger to keep myself from crying out.

He thrust his tongue inside me, then quickly withdrew, making me pant for more. With his left palm just below the base of my navel, he pressed down applying pressure to my belly as he entered me with his fingers while softly kissing the bud of my clitoris with his mouth. He gently swirled his tongue around as the intensity of the various pressures engulfed me into a fiery passion I never knew I was capable

40

of.

With a mind of its own, my pelvis quickly gripped him back without my permission. My vulnerability level was off the charts as my half lidded eyes began to close. "You like that, don't you, Angel?" He asked. My eyes were shut tight, but I could still hear that sexy smirk of his in his voice. I moaned my response, managing to spit out a shaky "Yes."

"I want to see your beautiful eyes, Angel... Look at me." He commanded as I tried my best to pry them open. My vision was still a bit blurry when I watched him remove his fingers from inside me and bring them to his mouth. "You taste so sweet, Baby." He said with a devilish grin, his eyes a brand new shade of violet. He cast his gaze directly into my own and licked the pad of his thumb, placing it on the bud of my clitoris as he worked it in slow rhythmic circles until I could no longer keep my cries of pleasure under control. My knees were beginning to shake as my body started to shudder beneath his touch. "That's it, Angel. Let yourself go," He said as he moved in for the kill. He pressed his wet thumb inside the brim of my behind while kissing my clitoris as if it were my mouth. Sliding his fingers in and out of me until I shamelessly cried out in ecstasy and ask for more.

"Jasper... Please..." I begged.

I was so consumed by my emotions, it felt like my heart could beat right out of my chest. I took a shallow breath in, forcing my mind clear of my own judgment and let myself go. "Come for me, Angel." Jasper said. How on earth those four little words he had spoken were all I needed to bring me to orgasm, was completely beyond my realm of understanding. My body trembled in waves as I found my release.

Jasper quickly stood up from the floor and went to the bathroom. I could hear the water running in the faucet as I lay there steadying my breath. A moment later, he produced a warm wet washcloth to dab me dry before climbing up on the bed to kiss my lips. He pulled me close to his chest and slid his hands down my shoulders. "That was for you, Angel. I can wait for mine. We need to get you up and ready for your appointment." *Boy was he right?* He damn sure made me forget about everything. I barely even knew my own name at that moment. I finally caught my breath when my pulse returned to its normal rhythm.

"So... what was that all about?" I asked, shyly into his strong shoulders. I was still too bashful to look into his eyes.

"I just want you to relax today. You've been through enough. You don't have to tell the detective about anything you don't feel comfortable with," Jasper replied.

"But I thought you said-" I started to say.

"I know what I said, and I meant it." I watched his Adam's apple rise and fall as he contemplated his next words. "I had a little chat with your ex this morning and I think we can agree that you pretty much have the upper hand here. If he doesn't get the help he needs, you can always give your statement to the police. You've been tormented enough." He said as he swiped away an unruly lock of hair from my eyes so he could implore them.

"You went to see AJ? This morning?" I asked, shocked by his revelation. I mean, it made perfect sense that Jasper would defend me, but I couldn't believe that he was actually willing to help him after everything I opened up to him about.

42

"Yes, I did. You were crying in your sleep, last night. I couldn't make out what you were saying, but it killed me to see you in distress at a time when you should have peace. I couldn't go back to sleep. I went over it so many times and it seems pretty clear to me that the biggest part of your torment lies within your conscience. You believe he can still be helped. This can be his second chance if he's smart enough to take it. I will see what can be done about his rehabilitation as long as he is willing to put in the work to help himself and he agrees to stay far away from you and your family. You're mine now Angel," Jasper declared. "That is, if you'll have me." The flash of his best puppy dog eyes had my heart aglow. "AJ knows that now, and is well aware that he fucked up any chance he had at having you. You deserve the world, Angel and I intend to give it my all to give that to you. Starting with this."

I couldn't believe, nor begin to process what I was hearing. "I see. But, what about Abby?" I asked.

"Abby can say whatever she chooses too, and AJ will have to reap whatever consequences that may come along with that. Same with you, Angel. You tell that detective anything your heart desires. I'm just letting you know that I am here to support you and whatever *you* decide to do. One thing I will promise, you and Abby will never have to deal with him again."

If I had any shred of doubt of my future with Jasper, everything he just stated to me was sure to banish it all away. The compassion inside his heart was the kind a person could journey their entire life to find. His ability to look beyond the surface of my suffering to pinpoint what my heart needed and what it would take for me to truly heal was a sign that he was deep down in the nitty gritty with me. He wanted my whole heart and was willing to do whatever it took to seal every single crack inside it. Never before, would I have fallen head over heels for someone I had just met, but our bond was far beyond extraordinary. Our undeniable love for each other was nothing short of fate's way of letting me know that this man was everything my imagination initially felt he was.

Chapter 8

I
t was nearly 11 AM when Abby came knocking on our hotel room door. Jasper and I were both dressed and ready to go.

"Good morning," Abby said, bursting into our room. "Are you guys ready? It's getting late."

"Yes." I replied. I pinched my cheeks as I glanced in the mirror on our way out. I was still nervous, but feeling much better about our appointment.

"Are we still gonna get something for breakfast? I'm starving!" Abby asked, as the three of us made our way to the elevator.

"Of course! We'll just have to get something on the road so we're not too late." Jasper replied.

"Did you guys see the cookies? OMG! They were so yummy! I made Mama try one but I finished the rest of them last night. They were so good!" Abby exclaimed. *Ahh! To be young and not have to worry about the unforgiving calories that came along with them.* I thought to myself. I was surprised that Abby appeared unaffected by the previous day's events.

"Yes, we saw them. I'll be sure to save you some of ours then, since you liked them so much!" It was the least I could do to make it up to her. I had a feeling Abby would be reaping the benefits of my guilt for quite some time.

"You two wait here while I go get the car." Jasper said as we stepped into the hotel lobby.

"Okay," I said as I watched him hurry out into the parking lot. This was the first time I was alone with Abby. I was curious to know if she was truly okay. She seemed to be handling things a lot better than I would have thought she would. "So how are you doing with all this?" I asked.

"I'm fine, Carla, truly I am. Like I said, I was more worried about you than anything. Besides, AJ was so drunk, I probably could have taken him down myself if it had come to that! Honestly, I was worried about what he might do to himself at one point. He seemed so depressed and I could barely make out what he was saying before he passed out," She replied. Abby was always strong. Her answer didn't surprise me, but just to be sure, I did want to keep my eye on her in case she was masking her true feelings like I tended to do.

When Jasper pulled up to the curb where we were waiting for him, he quickly hopped out of the rental car to open the doors for both of us. I still found his chivalry both surprising and sexy. These sweet little gestures only deepened my attraction to him. I think it was because it

46

was so different from the treatment I was used to having with AJ.

We stopped in at the drive-thru donut shop to grab our breakfast to go. The morning was quickly getting away from us and we wanted to make sure we got to the police station before it was too late. I made quick work of my egg and cheese English muffin since I had barely eaten my dinner the night before. Jasper devoured his bacon egg and cheese croissant. I couldn't help but notice how attractive he was even as I watched him eat his sandwich.

As if she could care less about her sugar intake, Abby had two donuts while I silently wondered to myself where she put it all. I swear this girl could eat whatever she wanted and never seemed to gain a single pound. *Ahh! To be a teenager again!* Even in my youth, I had to work extra hard to burn those extra calories off. Abby was always into sports though, so perhaps that's where it all went. The closest thing to sports I had ever engaged in was tap dancing when I was six and roller skating when I was closer to Abby's age, but I only went once or twice a month. I nearly cried when the skating rink closed down for good. The best of teenage memories lived in that rink!

Chapter 9

W e arrived at the police station a few minutes before noon. *Technically, it was still morning.* We were informed by the officer at the front desk that Detective Stacy was out getting her lunch and would soon be back in the office. Apparently, she'd left specific instructions for us to sit tight and wait for her return. By that time, my nerves were wound so tight that I made a full course meal out of removing the polish from my fingernails with my teeth while we sat in the row of seats aligning the exterior wall to the station.

The police station looked like something straight out of a seventies film. There were several desks married together in one large office with only a few feet of space in between each one, leaving no privacy to its user. I imagined it would have been quite the challenge for me to consider opening up to talk about my private issues while everyone stared at me. Even if they weren't paying me any mind, I would certainly feel like they were. I roamed my eyes around the room to find a few closed door offices aligning the back wall and silently hoped the detective would arrange one of the private rooms for us to use for our meeting.

At this point, I had settled on letting my instincts tell me what to do when the detective questioned me. If Jasper was right and we were able to facilitate the possibility of AJ going to rehab, I truly believed AJ had a chance at a good life, but only if he was ready and willing to accept the help that was given to him.

AJ had never been forthcoming about his past with his family. I knew his dad was in prison and that he primarily spent his childhood with his mom who harbored enough crap from men that she eventually gave up on them altogether. She was currently living with her girlfriend of ten years. I'd only met her a time or two because AJ wasn't very close with his mom, but he never told me why. I was sure it had something to do with whatever reason he had to leave home when he was only 16.

The truth was, AJ's secrets are what kept me drawn to him. There was so much behind his facade that mystified me. An enigma I was all too curious to figure out. At times, I found it infuriating when he would act so macho in the presence of his so called friends. I never felt like any of them had his best intentions at heart because they only seemed to show up when it was time to party. It was the act, alone, that bothered me so much. To me, it had always been crystal clear that the mask AJ hid behind was a wall of self defense. When anyone came too close, he would shut them out entirely.

After getting to know Jasper, I realized I had gained far more insight as to who he was in the short time we'd known each other than I was ever able to learn about AJ in the entire two years we were a couple. I knew enough now to be sure that whether AJ recovered or not, I no longer desired to be with him. Even though I was royally pissed at him for dragging Abby into the drama of our relationship, I still cared very deeply about his well being.

At the end of the row of chairs from where we were seated, a young woman who appeared to be about my age was sitting with a baby on her arm and a young boy of maybe 3 or 4 years old. The toddler had a clear injury to his arm that was dressed in a dark blue sling. With streaks of mascara running down her face, it was apparent that she was distraught. She had bruises trailing up her arm where the baby was drooling. It was my guess that she was waiting to report domestic violence.

My heart ached for her. Her troubled eyes told me she was just as lost as I had been when I first left AJ. The only difference between us was that she was not alone. She had children who needed her to be strong. I couldn't imagine how awful it would have been to have had a child witness the situations I had been in. Even worse, if they had to suffer the abuse along with me. Even though my heart truly wanted to see AJ recover, that didn't mean I wouldn't be wise to protect myself against him. Taking Abby was much further than I ever would have expected him to take things. I let a sigh pass my lips at my thoughts.

Jasper placed his hands in mine and gave it a gentle squeeze. "It's going to be OK, Angel, we are right here with you." He said, reassuringly just as Detective Stacy walked through the door holding a brown paper bag that likely contained the lunch she had gone out for. I could smell the french fries a mile away. She must have been notified that we were there while she was out because she was headed straight for us.

~

Detective Stacy invited Abby to follow her to one of the private rooms. Since Abby was over the age of 16, the law allowed for her to be questioned without a parent present. This was good news because even though Mama really wanted to be here for us, she had other obligations back home that couldn't be rescheduled. With Abby going first, I was more than relieved to see we didn't have to give our statements at one of the exposed desks.

Evidently, Abby demanded to ride in the ambulance with me when they brought me to the emergency room. She had given most of her statement right beforehand, so Detective Stacy already had most of what she needed of Abby from the day prior. When Abby soon returned to where we were sitting, I knew that I would be next. Jasper extended his warmth around me in a quick embrace before I stood up to follow the detective.

As we made our way down the center aisle of desks, I couldn't help but wish I could just disappear into thin air. The emotions that crept into my core had my stomach twisted in knots. With images of the scorned woman and her teary eyed babies in my mind along with the whisper of Jasper's wisdom from overcoming his own demons echoing in my ear, I was awakened to the need to seek the justice I had come here for.

Like a mother who hated having to discipline her child, my heart was breaking for AJ and what I feared would soon be at his doorstep. If I let him off the hook for everything he'd done to me, he would never learn from his mistakes. He would never understand the suffering he'd caused me without having knowledge of the damage he'd done. And without my statement in its sincerity, I knew there could be no acceptance and moving on for him. It was time for me to stand in my truth.

I honestly believed AJ was blinded by the haze of his alcoholism the whole time we were together and held no capacity to truly comprehend my emotions until he dealt with the ones that he, himself, had been stuffing into each bottle he set his lips upon.

The tall, blue eyed, dark blonde detective closed the door behind us and directed me to sit down as she took her own seat on the other side of the table. The gray metal chair was cold to the touch, as was the air inside the room. On top of the table between Detective Stacy and me, there was a glass of water and a box of tissues. She offered me the glass of water before proceeding to ask me the questions she needed for her report.

By the time we were finished, she had full knowledge of the situation between AJ and me and I had made use of both the water and tissues. We also filed a restraining order against AJ. Although it tore me to shreds, knowing how powerful my statement would be in a case against AJ, I told her everything she needed to know for her report. Mama and Joel always taught me that "honesty was the best policy," and these were words I had chosen to live by. Accountability was where AJ would learn from his mistakes. Just as I had learned that beyond being honest, not withholding the truth was just as important.

The officer followed close behind me to meet Jasper and Abby who were both patiently waiting for us to finish our meeting. Jasper quickly stood up and extended his hand out to Detective Stacy.

"Hello officer, I'm Jasper, Carla's... friend. I was hoping we could have a word, if that's alright?" Jasper asked the detective while taking in my reaction. I gave him a quick nod to let him know I was onboard with what we had discussed about helping AJ's case.

"Sure thing." Detective Stacy replied.

"Is there a number where my lawyer can be in contact with you regarding AJ's case?" Jasper asked. An expression of confusion quickly flashed across the officer's face.

"I don't understand. *You* want to hire a lawyer for *AJ?*

"Yes." Jasper replied, wrapping his arm around my shoulder.

"We think he might benefit from some leniency and would like to request that he be considered for a rehabilitation program if that's possible."

"I see." She said, eyeing my reaction to Jasper's offer to help AJ.

"I honestly don't think he would ever have treated me the way he did had he not been drinking. He hasn't been himself, these past few months. I believe there is something more behind his addiction that needs to surface before he can truly heal and I'm afraid he will only get worse if he doesn't get some help." I offered to solidify Jasper's statement.

"I see. I will add this to your statement. I am not sure what can be done, it would depend on what the judge sees fit, but wait here a minute." The officer replied before walking over to her desk to produce a business card for Jasper. "You can have your lawyer call if you want him to represent AJ and we'll just have to wait and see what happens. I know this wasn't an easy thing for you to do, Miss Taylor. Thank you for your time. I will be in touch if anything else comes up." The detective said as she walked us to the door.

Chapter 10

We left the police station and headed back towards the hotel. With an unabated obligation to call Jamie tapping at my shoulder, I asked Jasper to stop at the local drug store where I could buy myself a new cell phone charger. I let my mind rest on the knowledge that Mama had at least given her an update. I was sure that Jamie would not have had a wink of sleep, had she not heard anything by now. In all honesty, I really needed my best friend.

Jasper refused to let me pay for my charger. I found his gesture endearing, but I also wasn't used to being taken care of by someone, like him. Normally, my pride would have stepped in the way and wouldn't have backed down, but those spellbinding blue eyes of his had my resistance crumbling at every turn. In spite of my pride, his nurturing side only strengthened my attraction to him.

I found myself daydreaming as I peered my eyes out onto the open road ahead of us on our drive back to the hotel. The sky was overcast with various shades of gray in the clouds. The autumn colored leaves of the trees were beginning to blow off with the wind. My stomach began to churn with longing at the recollection of how aroused I was when Jasper woke me up, earlier that day. Suddenly, that deeply fostered violet shade of blue I had seen in his eyes when I climaxed resurfaced in my mind. I was quickly awakened to his hunger for me, as it unleashed into the wild like a wolf on the hunt until I fed him with my release.

"Are we still gonna get lunch? I'm more tired than hungry." Abby asked from the back seat, yanking me away from my wayward thoughts.

"I wouldn't mind getting some rest, how about you, Angel? We can go for dinner instead if you want." Jasper offered. *I could do more than just rest!* I mischievously thought to myself. What I really wanted was to even the score from earlier that morning.

"A nap sounds like a great idea!" I quickly agreed before I let on to just how far down in the gutter my mind had gone. With Abby in the car, my wants would sorely have to take a back seat to what I truly needed in that moment. Reluctantly, I brought myself back into the presence of my company to respond. "I have to charge my phone and call Jamie anyway. We'll just have to let Mama know that you'll be home a little later than we expected." I added.

"Ooh, maybe she'll let me stay another day! Can we ask her?" Abby asked, excitedly. Jasper turned his head in my direction to exchange glances with me. I could see through his eyes, he was clearly on Abby's side. It was difficult for me to say "no" to Abby. Especially after all she'd been through on account of my mistakes. I let myself cave into the idea that Abby could probably use a personal day off from school to recuperate from everything.

"I don't see why not?" I replied, feeling grateful for my response the moment I saw the smile spread across Abby's face through the rear view mirror.

"I'll see if we can extend your room for another night. I'm sure it won't be a problem." Jasper reiterated to Abby as we pulled into the parking lot of the hotel. He dropped us both off at the entrance and went to park the car in the lot.

As Abby and I waited for Jasper to return, she turned to me and said, "I really like your new boyfriend, he's so nice... A major upgrade from AJ if you ask me!" I immediately started to blush and couldn't help but wonder if Abby was forming a little crush of her own. *The least of my worries.* As lucky as I felt to have Jasper swooning over me, the idea of batting other women off him did have my stomach tied up a bit. There was no denying the fact that he was a certified hottie! Not that I saw Abby as a threat anyway. I knew she'd never do something like that to me, I had no doubt in my trust in her. Besides, she was nearly a dozen years younger than him, anyway. *But what about the others?* I quickly tucked that thought away the moment I saw his gorgeous face coming our way.

~

We had no trouble extending the rooms for another night. After stopping by the gift shop to buy Abby some new clothes to change into, we dropped her off at her room so she could rest. As soon as we entered our own room, I made a beeline to the table where I left my dead phone and plugged it in to charge. As soon as it lit up, I quickly shot out a text to Jamie.

Me:

Hey Jamie, I'm okay! I'm so sorry for leaving without saying anything. Please don't be mad at me! I'll give you a call later this evening!

I didn't expect her to reply right away as she would more than likely be in class. I felt terrible for not keeping her in the loop of what was going on, especially since she had welcomed me into her home with open arms and was there for me the entire time I was in Boston. I was surprised when my phone instantly chimed back.

Jamie:

Thank God you're OK! Please don't worry yourself about it! I'm in class right now, talk laters, k?

My entire body relaxed the moment I read her text. Just knowing that she knew I was alright relieved a great deal of the tension I was feeling. I couldn't wait to talk to her later that evening to help her get caught up in the current drama that was surrounding my existence.

"I'm going to take a shower. Why don't you lie down and get some rest for a while before we go to dinner. I won't be long," Jasper said, as he quickly stripped the clothes away from his gorgeous body all the way down to his boxer shorts. I instantly felt the heat pooling inside my cheeks and quickly turned away. Jasper chuckled at my not so smooth reaction and stalked his way over to me to tug my chin in his direction. He stared directly into my eyes and kissed me.

"You're going to have to get used to seeing me naked, Angel." He whispered into my lips. "Not that I don't thoroughly enjoy watching you squirm," He teased as he tossed me his boxers before heading into the bathroom. I let out a huge sigh and fell back on the bed. My mind was still swimming in bliss with the pleasure he had ever so kindly delivered to the front door of my waking moments, earlier that day.

The butterflies all waved their wings in the air before dipping down the track as I slipped into euphoric state of consciousness. I was fast asleep when Jasper rippled his way under the covers and wrapped his arms around me. With my eyes remaining closed, I trickled my fingers across the soft hairs of his forearm. His skin felt leathery soft against my finger tips. He pulled me closer and I could feel his erection springing against my back. In my dreamy state, I felt blissfully uninhibited by my conscience. Splaying my free hand down, across the upper portion of his thigh, I slowly turned to face him. "Hi." I said with a small smile as I slowly willed my eyes to flutter open.

He quickly kissed my lips, igniting the passion within me to a blazing fire. I kissed him back with everything I had inside me, slowly skating my hands down his beautifully sculpted chest to explore each and every ripple of his physique. Jasper smoothed his fingers through my hair and released it at my shoulder, momentarily parting from my lips to burn a hole straight through me with his eager, hungry eyes. He quickly pressed his lips back onto mine, exchanging his own desire with my own. I let my hands boldly make their way down to lightly brush over his erection, then quickly retreated to his belly. Jasper found my hands beneath the covers. He laced his fingers through mine and quickly guided them back. "You want this, Angel?" He asked. "All you ever have to do is ask. I will never deny you of your needs," He said.

I replied with a sultry kiss upon his lips, then broke away to daringly slide my tongue across the Adam's apple of his throat. Planting soft kisses down his deliciously chiseled chest, I briefly stopped to admire the happy trail that led down to his navel. Empowered by the disguise of the blanket that covered me, matched with my uninhibited dreamy state of consciousness, I permitted myself to return this morning's favor to him. I slowly tugged at the upper rim of his boxer shorts and he quickly sprang free for me to see what I was working with. He was deliciously perfect! Large enough for pleasure without being too overwhelming in size . I slowly let my tongue swirl around his tip in a playful tease. Jasper gently gripped the back of my neck in a silent plea for me to continue what I had started. I slid my tongue down the base of his penis, and back up to swirl the tip again. With Jasper's throaty groans fueling my desire, I plunged down to take in the full length of his shaft.

"Fuck! You're pretty mouth feels so good around my cock, Angel... Please don't stop!" He cried out in pleasure, making me aim to please him even more.

I palmed his base with my hand in a slow pumping motion as I continued to work my tongue at his tip. Jasper's moaning increased as he quickly pushed his hands down to where my mouth was to stop me. He nudged me, pulling my body up so I could be face to face with him. I peeped my head out of the covers to stare directly into the fire of his deep blue violet eyes. "I need your lips on me now," Jasper groaned as he feverishly pressed his lips onto mine, unleashing that familiar passion I had been longing for behind his kiss. Jasper continued the dance of our tongues as he blindly reached over to the nightstand where he'd left his wallet. He fumbled his way to the condom inside and tore it open before sliding it down onto his fully erect penis.

"You can climb on top now if you want, Angel," He huffed.

"I've never been on top before," I replied, shyly.

"Don't worry, baby, I will guide you through it. You can do me no wrong, I promise you that!" He said with a reassuring laugh.

And as he commanded, I mounted myself on top of his thighs as he grabbed hold of my hips and guided himself into me. Pushing and pulling my hips up and down as I caught a rhythm that was pleasing to us both. He playfully nipped at my hardened nipples with his mouth. Pausing to praise me. "You're seriously are a goddess, Angel. So fucking beautiful!" he said as he smoothed his hands through the long auburn waves of my hair beside my breasts. "I like having you ride me, Angel. I can take in the full view of your beauty and watch those pretty eyes of yours." He said, making me moan even louder as he slowly brought his hands down to work the bud of my clitoris between his fingers tips.

"I want to see the pleasure in your eyes when I make you come. Let yourself Go, Angel." I closed my eyes and pumped my body faster and faster, rocking back and forth as his grip on me let me escape to the realm of my own little world of fantasy. A place where nothing else mattered but Jasper's undivided attention on me.

I was on the brink of my release when Jasper began matching my rhythm with his own. His fingers between my legs, gently moving faster to meet our pace as my imagination was lost somewhere deep in the sweet wonderland of the mystical forest I had previously dreamt of. This time, I was riding a unicorn in search of the glowing river to find Jasper. Just as I reached the bank of the river, I heard him calling out my name.

"Carla... My sweet Angel... Open your eyes for me."

The second I opened my eyes, he pressed the pad of his thumb into my clitoris as if it were some magic button that had the power to immediately claim my orgasm with his own. I felt my body shutter as my breath hitched inside his. He stared deep into my eyes, and passionately kissed my mouth deeper than ever before. With my heart pounding and the clamminess of our skin pressed together as we were both drenched in the sweat we were producing, I let my head rest against his chest to find that my heart was not alone in this race.

"My beautiful Angel," Jasper said in a breathy chuckle as he smoothed his hand over my head. "For the record, I never would have guessed that this was your first time on top." He said with his signature smirk as we both lay there catching our breath in each other's arms.

My body was spent. My emotions were all consuming, like a pirate who'd found his long journeyed treasure. As I lay there on his chest, taking everything in, I wondered if I should pinch myself to see if I was dreaming. This incredibly hot guy lying beneath me was everything I had ever wanted in a man. Loving, protective, supportive and one hell of a lover. The icing to my cake of dreams. I lapped this rush of dopamine up like a long lost puppy who'd finally found his way home and fell fast asleep in the comfort of Jasper's arms.

Chapter 11

⁓ ❦ ⁓

The curtains were drawn tight in our hotel room, as I lay awake in bed. Jasper was no longer beside me. With no light of day in the room, I was clueless as to what time it was. I slipped myself out from underneath the covers to check the time on my phone. It was nearly 6 o'clock. I listened closely to hear the faint chatter of Jasper's voice coming from outside on the balcony. I drew the curtain open to find him sitting on the chair talking on his cell phone. When I opened the door, his expression fell on me like a dark cloud. Something was wrong, I could see it in his eyes.

"Okay, thank you. Bye," Jasper said, as he quickly ended the phone call he was on. "Hey Angel, I'm so sorry to do this, especially on your birthday, but I have an urgent matter I need to tend to back home." I could feel his energy shifting and though I was curious, I knew that whatever it was, it wasn't something he was comfortable sharing with me. So I dared not to ask.

"I have a flight to catch in a few hours and I'm afraid I won't be able to take you to dinner as we planned tonight." The expression on his face, laden with guilt as he paused before asking, "Would it be alright with you if I brought you to your car so you'll be able to take Abby home?" It didn't matter to me whether he took me to dinner or not, it was a nice gesture, of course, but I was more devastated to see him leave than anything else.

"Of course!" I replied politely.

"I will make it up to you, Angel, I promise!" He said as he opened the sliding glass door a little further to let himself inside. "I'm going to leave you my credit card. I want you and Abby to go wherever you like for dinner-"

"Oh, no you don't have to-" I started to say, when Jasper reached over to put his finger over my mouth.

"Shh... I won't take no for an answer and please feel free to use it as you wish for anything you need while you're here. I want you and Abby to have a good time and I want you to find something a little more suitable than 'gift shop finds' for a birthday gift for yourself." He pulled his wallet out of his pocket to produce the credit card he had mentioned. "The limit on this one is only 15 thousand, but I'm sure it will be enough to suit your needs until you get back home to Boston. If for some reason you need more, please just let me know." I was dumbfounded, knowing he was entrusting me with the use of his credit. At first, I said nothing in return, but the look in his eyes penetrated through me, daring me to challenge him in his time of unease. "Promise me, Angel. You'll let me know."

I could tell that he needed to know that I was going to be okay, regardless of whatever was ailing him back home. So I agreed. "I promise." I said in a deep exhale of my forgotten breath.

~

"So we're not going to dinner?" Abby whined as she flashed her puppy dog eyes up at me
    from underneath the covers, instantly casting me into a world of guilt.

"I didn't say that, but Jasper has to fly back to Boston. We're going to dinner after he brings us back to my old apartment so I can pick up my car. Now can you please go get dressed so he won't miss his flight?" I pleaded. I was guilty, yes! But I was equally annoyed at having to explain everything before I could even get Abby out of bed to get ready. I pulled the covers down off of her in a sudden attempt to get things moving.

"Okay, fine!" She yelled back, "You don't have to be so dramatic!" Thankfully, she took the hint and got up to make her way to the bathroom to get dressed while I sat in the arm chair in the corner of the room. I shot out a text to Jamie while I was waiting.

Me:

Hey, I didn't forget about you, I promise I will call you later tonight. I have so much to tell you! xo

Jamie:

No worries, Sounds good! Talk laters! Xo

After a few minutes, Abby finally came out of the bathroom dressed in her new blue and white floral sundress we had bought her from the gift shop. I had to admit, the dress looked really cute on her. So much that I was toying with the idea of buying one for myself in a different color.

My phone rang just as we were leaving Abby's room. It was Jasper calling to let me know he was already packed and waiting in the car downstairs, just outside the lobby. When we passed by the gift shop, I figured it best to wait until the morning to buy the dress so Jasper wouldn't be late to the airport.

Chapter 12

W e arrived at my old apartment to pick up my car a few minutes after 7. Jasper's flight was scheduled to depart at 9:45 so he had to leave in a hurry.

"I'm gonna miss that Angel face of yours." He whispered in my ear as he was leaving. My body trembled in anticipation of our departing embrace but I could feel the absence of his passion in our kiss, goodbye. Whatever he was facing was definitely eating away at him. I could feel it in his energy. "I'll call you later tonight." He said with a small smile. It was clearly an attempt on his part to keep me from worrying too much about whatever it was that he was dealing with.

"Okay, get home safe!" I called out to him as Abby and I watched him drive off into the night. I felt very uneasy about the way he left. I would have been totally fine with him leaving for Lucas, or work, or anything else, had I known that everything would be alright. Still, I knew I couldn't keep him here with me while I dealt with what I needed to. I felt deeply obligated to ensure that Abby was truly okay before I could pick up and leave to go back to Boston. It appeared that she was handling things well, but I figured I would hang around for a week or so just to be sure. With AJ in police custody, I knew that this was probably the only safe time to recover my belongings without having to see him.

"Come on, I could use your help." I said to Abby when we pulled into the parking lot of my old apartment.

"What are we doing?" Abby asked.

"I need to grab some things, while AJ's gone." I replied.

Abby followed me down the old familiar path I used to dread walking home upon. We were met with balloons and party streamers and an eerie feeling when we entered my old apartment. The air was stagnantly perfumed with the faint smell of Jack Daniels. For the first time ever, it didn't feel like home anymore. I almost felt like a criminal walking into my own apartment.

The 30-day notice sitting on the kitchen counter confirmed the fact that AJ wasn't keeping up with the rent. In my heart, I knew he wouldn't be able to support his addiction and pay the bills on his measly little check from unemployment. It was a big part of the reason why I felt so guilty for leaving the way I had. The truth was, even though I felt partially responsible for AJ's suffering, he was still a grown man who was more than capable of taking care of business on his own. The problem was, he had to want it for himself.

He stopped looking for work the moment he began drinking on a daily basis. No matter how supportive I tried to be, it seemed like nothing I did was ever enough. Looking back, I think I may have done him more harm than good by picking up his slack without pressuring him to find a new job. But that was all in the past now and I was desperately trying to lend myself some grace. It was never my intention to lead us to the road we were on, only to wind up taking the high road out.

"I'm just going to pack some clothes and grab a few essential things," I said to Abby, as I caught her turning her nose up at the stench. It was clear to me, she didn't want to be here anymore than I did.

"Okay, just tell me what you need me to do." She said.

"Can you do me a favor and go in the closet near the bathroom and look for a black safe, please. It should be up on the top shelf," I said as I headed for the bedroom to find my old suitcase.

"Okay," Abby replied.

I grabbed most of my clothes that were hanging in the closet, my Raggedy Ann Doll that my Grandma bought me before she passed away and all of my old photo albums and tossed it all onto the bed. There was no way I would fit it all inside the suitcase.

"Hey Squirt, can you come here please?" I called out to Abby.

Abby quickly appeared in the doorway holding the safe I asked her to grab for me. Thankfully the safe was small as it mainly held my important documents, like my high school diploma, birth certificate and a few old poems and short stories I'd written in high school. I loaded the safe on top of everything else and attempted to get it closed with no success.

"Okay, clearly this isn't working…. Can you sit on top so I can zip it please?" I asked. Abby quickly adhered to my request and jumped up on the bed to hover over the suitcase with her rear. With Abby's weight on top, holding it down, I was finally able to zip it closed.

"Teamwork makes the dream work!" Abby said with a sarcastic grin spread across her face as she jumped down off the bed.

"Okay, I just need to find something to pack my shoes in and we can get out of here," I said.

"I know, we can just use your laundry basket, I saw it in the kitchen." Abby offered.

"Good thinking!" I said as I headed toward the kitchen to grab it. I was quickly reminded of the night I had finally had enough and made the decision to leave. That night had definitely been the straw that broke the camel's back. I couldn't help from recalling how much I had cried that night, so much that there were no more tears left to produce. Suddenly it dawned on me that my decision to leave was more than likely the best decision I could have ever made. *Wow! What a difference a few weeks and a change in perspective can make?*

I scooped up the laundry basket from off the kitchen floor that looked like it hadn't been washed since the time I'd left and quickly gathered the shoes I wanted to take with me. Everything else that was there could remain, for all I cared. I was over my relationship with AJ, or at the very least, I was telling myself I was, despite the fact that I still cared about his well being. Something inside me knew that I was done with him for good the moment he brought Abby into this. It was a low blow, even for AJ. He knew very well just how much she meant to me. And I honestly didn't care what his intentions were. Putting Abby at stake was a move I had no other choice but to fold my hand for, regardless of what cards I may have held inside my hands.

"Well, I guess this is it!" I said, taking a quick look around the apartment that AJ and I called home for 8 torturous months. It wasn't like I had any friends here. Only a few passing respectful smiles had been exchanged between myself and my neighbors. I was often too embarrassed by AJ's lack of respect to be friendly, anyway.

With Abby's help, we were able to make it back to my car in one trip so I locked the door behind us. I stopped to think about AJ's stuff and what would happen to it all if he hadn't been released from the police before they came to clean out the apartment.

If he had been any closer to his mom, I would have extended him the courtesy of letting her know what was happening so she could come and collect his things for him. But AJ was distant with her, and I didn't even have a number to reach her. I had to let it go. AJ and his belongings were no longer my responsibility.

Chapter 13

I t was already getting late and most of the restaurants would soon be closed for the night. Abby and I decided to order room service at the hotel for dinner. As someone who worked in the service industry, I was more than familiar with how annoying it was to have someone walk through the door at closing time while I was trying to finish my side work. The last thing I wanted was to be *those people!*

We got back to the hotel just after 9 PM. Abby found the menu for room service in the drawer and began reading it off to me as I slipped out of my cami and into the t-shirt Jasper bought me from the gift shop the day prior. I was quickly reminded of the cupcakes we never had the chance to indulge in that were still left sitting over on the nightstand. I was sure that Abby would be happy to help me out with them after dinner.

"I'm gonna order the Chicken Parmesan, what do you want?" Abby asked.

"The shrimp scampi sounds good, with Fettuccine Alfredo for my side, please," I replied.

My phone pinged with a text message notification. I quickly grabbed it out of my purse thinking it might be Jasper, but it wasn't.

Brooke:

Hey! What happened to you today? Shit! With everything going on, I had completely forgotten I was scheduled to work at the coffee shop! I wasn't ready to spill everything to Brooke just yet, I needed to talk to Jamie first so I could try to begin processing everything that happened.

Me:

OMG! I forgot to call into work, this morning. I had a family emergency and had to leave town. It's a long story. I'll have to explain later. Can you please let Ben know I'm sorry. Tell him that I will be in touch with him tomorrow.

Brooke:

Okay. Hope everything's alright.

Me:

It will be, but I will need to stay here for a little bit longer. Please work your charm on Ben. Tell him not to fire me, please! I really need this job.

Brooke:

I'll see what I can do, he was pretty pissed this morning. You know he's not a fan of actual work.

Me:

Shit you're right. Lol But still! I have faith in you, you got this!💯 I'll talk to you soon! Thanks 😊

Jasper's flight was scheduled to leave soon. I figured I might still have enough time to shoot him a quick text message before he boarded the plane.

Me:

Have a safe trip home. Miss you already.

Jasper:

Thanks. I'll call you when I get back.

Even in his text message, I could feel the shift in his energy. He was detached. Whatever was going on in his world, that I seemed to be no part of, certainly had his attention. I had to let it go or that bitch called anxiety would creep her ugly face back into my mind.

The truth was, I already had enough to process in my own little world and what I needed the most right now was my best friend. I needed to talk to Jamie. I needed her to know that I was going to be okay, but I also wanted to hear what she thought about what was going on between Jasper and me and the space that we were currently in. I made myself comfortable in the arm chair next to the sliding glass door and dialed Jamie's number.

Jamie must have been waiting on my call because she picked up on the second ring. I brought her up to speed on everything that had transpired since I left Boston. I spared her the dirty details of the intimacy Jasper and I shared, while leaving enough to her imagination to catch my drift.

"I don't know, Carla. It could be anything, but it definitely sounds serious. I honestly can't believe that AJ would do this to you. Then again, I also had no idea he was treating you so badly all this time. Maybe I shouldn't be surprised at all. Did you file a restraining order?" She asked.

"Yes, I did," I said, sighing as I shifted my thoughts from Jasper back to AJ. I knew Jamie would be proud that I went through with it. "Putting Abby at stake was the last straw. I mean, I feel for him, I really do, because I know somewhere deep within the walls he's surrounded himself with, there's a lost boy inside who is desperate to be saved," I replied.

"It is not your job to rescue him," Jamie quickly interjected. "He's a grown ass man who has put you through more shit than I ever would've stuck around for. You have to take care of yourself, Carla. And that goes without the mention of the gorgeous hottie, who not only *wants* to be with you, but treats you like the queen you are, girl. From where I stand, there's really no decision to be made here," She said. I wasn't at all surprised by her stance on the situation. I just really needed her to give it to me straight, just as I knew she would.

Honestly, she really shouldn't have had to convince me because we were talking about the difference between a McDonald's hamburger and filet mignon, in terms of the treatment I had received by AJ and Jasper. My tummy began to grumble at my own choice of metaphors as I briefly wondered how long it would take for our dinner to arrive.

"You're so right, Jamie. Believe it or not, I really am trying to get better at putting my own needs first. But you know me. You know I have a soft spot for people who are suffering…. I know, he won't ever admit to it, but I just know there's something eating away at AJ. Something very dark has brought him to where he is now. I don't want you to mistake my compassion for him as wanting to be with him, though. That ship has definitely sailed. I'm so angry about everything he's not only put me through, but now Abby, too! All I want is to see him get better, so I can move on with my life and see my way through whatever this is between Jasper and me."

"Well, I'm impressed by your strength and determination to grow from your experience, Carla. And I'm happy to hear that you and Abby are both okay. My personal opinion, AJ doesn't deserve your compassion. What he needs-is to grow the hell up!" I could hear the anger in her voice. I knew she had every right to be angry. I would be livid if someone had put her through everything I'd been through with AJ. Knowing that, I couldn't disagree with the point she was trying to make.

"I can't argue with you on that, Jamie, because you're right-" I started to say when I heard a knock on the door. "Listen Jamie, our food is here and I don't have any pants on. Can I call you back sometime tomorrow?" I asked as I scurried my way across the room to hide in the bathroom, all while motioning at Abby to answer the door for our dinner.

"Of course! Go eat!" She said, laughing at the picture I had painted of my current status.

"Okay, I'll talk to you soon!" I said before disconnecting the call. I stood there inside the bathroom listening through the door to make sure that whoever delivered our food was gone before walking out into the room.

"You can come out now, he's gone." Abby said as she licked the garlic off her fingers from the roll she had in her hand. The aroma hit my nose, and my mouth began to water. I was starving and could not wait to dive into my dinner.

"It smells delicious!" I said as I took a seat on the bed, holding the foil tin filled with fettuccine and shrimp. It was hot and beginning to burn my hand from holding on to it. I carefully placed it beside the box of cupcakes on the nightstand as I scoured the bag for utensils and napkins.

"Oh my God, it's so good!" Abby said, amused as she knifed her way into her Chicken Parmesan. "I'm so glad we decided to stay in, tonight. I don't think there is a restaurant around here that can compare to how good this is." Watching Abby enjoy her meal made me feel happy, inside.

"Me too. You're right, I never had any restaurants around here that have food this good, either! I guess it pays to stay at a quality hotel," I agreed. reminding myself to thank Jasper for dinner when I talked to him later that evening.

After dinner, Abby and I shared the cupcakes Jasper had bought me for my birthday. Watching her devour it almost made up for the fact that Jasper wasn't here to enjoy them with me.

After watching Abby flip through the channels for a while, I set my phone down on the charger, checking to make sure I hadn't missed a call from Jasper. By now, his plane should have already landed. Under normal circumstances, I would probably have called him to make sure that he arrived safely, but I honestly felt like he needed his space. So instead, I left the ball in his court to call me like he said he would.

"Well, I'm getting kind of tired and there's only one bed in this room... I think I'll go back to mine for the night since Jasper's paying for the extension anyway," Abby said. I had to chuckle at the recollection of the last time Abby and I had shared a bed. We were on vacation, as kids. I wound up on the floor because Abby had apparently kicked me off the bed while she slept. "Will you be alright here by yourself for the night?" She asked, looking concerned.

"I'll be fine. I prefer to sleep in the bed, anyway, not the floor," I teased. Abby giggled and poked my arm as she recalled my reference. She never woke up that night, but Joel and I both teased her for it the whole next day. "I'll walk you to your room." I said.

"Okay." She agreed before we both stood up and left for Abby's room.

Chapter 14

I fell asleep, waiting on a call from Jasper that never came. Instead, I awoke at 3 AM to find a text message that he must have sent just after I had fallen asleep.

Jasper

Hi Angel. It's pretty late, and I just got in. I'll call you tomorrow. Sleep well.

I'll admit, I was a little sad he didn't call me, but his chosen term of endearment for me, *Angel,* always had a way of awakening the butterflies within me. I was relieved to learn he made it home safe and wrapped myself in the cozy blanket of the butterfly sensations that would lull me back to sleep until morning.

The hotel room phone rang promptly at 9 AM. It was Abby calling to let me know she was up, ready and coming over. A quick glance at my phone revealed the fact I wasn't the first thing on Jasper's mind this morning. Jasper seemed to be an early riser from what I had seen of him so far. The truth was, even though I had yet to discover everything about him, I still felt an intense, almost telepathic connection to his energy.

The last thing I needed right now was to dwell on whether he was thinking about me or not. In fact, I had some pressing matters of my own to tend to. Like calling Ben and Maggie to beg them to let me keep my jobs back in Boston. I honestly felt sick to my stomach for not having called them yet. I could only pray they might be understanding of the fact that I had a family emergency. I hoped they would allow me some personal time to be able to sort things out.

Deciding who to call first wasn't very difficult since I was sure that Ben would be more of a challenge to convince. Especially after the charade of dramatics he used to complain about Peggy when I had first applied for the job. She was the girl whose shift I had taken over at the coffee shop.

It was painfully obvious of how annoyed he was at her leaving to be home with her newborn baby. He made it very clear how much her personal life had inconvenienced him. And since it was well after the start time of my shift... I already knew he was gonna be pissed. I could only hope that Brooke relayed my message to soften the delivery before I would talk to him, myself.

I let out a deep sigh as I reluctantly picked up my cell phone to dial Ben's number. When he didn't pick up my call, I was pleased to have the opportunity to leave a message on his voicemail, which would inadvertently give him some time to cool off before we spoke in person.

I had yet to be on the receiving end of one of Ben's rants, but I was sure it was a cold 1 from hell. With quick and clever thinking, I added in my message that cell service was spotty here in the mountains. I was planting the seed of an escape route, just in case he decided to call me back at a time when I didn't feel strong enough to brave the storm of his wrath.

The situation with Maggie was a little different. She was warmer and much more compassionate. That was obvious from the first day I met her. My job at Silver Linings, though merely a receptionist position, was far more important to me than my job at the coffee shop and I fully intended to do whatever it took to keep it. The job did have potential for growth and truly had my heart in its mission. It also kept me in connection with Jasper, despite whatever challenges that might have been lying ahead of us.

Maggie clearly put her heart and soul into her work and I just knew she would be far more understanding of my current circumstances, especially with the nature of the business she was in at Silver Linings. I had to keep in mind that regardless of how much she may have sympathized with my situation, my position could still very much be at stake after being very recently employed there. All the strain would be left on her in my absence and she was already far behind in her own work. That was how I landed the job in the first place.

I hated the fact that I was beginning my career with Silver Linings on such a shaky start. I wasn't going down without a fight though and was willing to do whatever she needed of me in an effort to make up for any inconvenience my situation may have caused her.

After some careful reflection of what I might say to Maggie, I searched for her number in my phone to give her a call. Just as I had found her number, Abby knocked on the door and my phone chimed in with a text message notification at the same time.

I set my phone down on the bed and went to open the door for Abby. She was carrying the gift shop bag with her clothes and I was briefly reminded of the sundress I had my eye on. While I did bring most of my clothes from my old apartment, I had left them all in the car. I suddenly remembered how intent Jasper seemed to be at buying me something for my birthday, so I sent Abby down to the gift shop with Jasper's credit card to buy the dress for me to wear. In Abby's departure, I retracted back to the bed to see who it was that texted me.

Jasper:

Good morning, Angel. I spoke to Maggie this morning. I had to tell her about everything, so I could convince her to let you keep your job. She wants you to take the week off and to let you know that your job will be waiting for you when you get back.

The news Jasper delivered left me both shocked and relieved. In a perfect world, I would have loved to discuss it with him first, but I also understood that he may have been caught in the moment with her and not knowing what to say. The fact that he went to bat for me left me with a pull in my core I had been longing for ever since he left to head back to Boston. It also had me wondering if he'd mentioned our relationship to her as well.

Me:

Wait... So does she know about us too?

Jasper must have been busy because I never received a reply. When Abby returned to the room, I quickly showered and got dressed so we could be out of the rooms by check out time. A glance in the mirror had me feeling confident enough to snap a quick selfie in my new dress to send to Jasper. The mid-thigh length, spaghetti strap sundress was forest green with little white flowers. It fit me well at the waist, and flared out at the skirt.

Me:

Thank you for my birthday gift, I hope you like it! ;) **(I captioned with the photo)**

Once again, no reply from Jasper. I didn't hear back from Jasper until later that evening while we were having dinner with Mama in her apartment.

Jasper:

Suits you very well ;) I can't wait to take you out in it and also out of it when you get back. His words had me blushing, so much that I had to sneak away from the dinner table where Abby, Mama and I were all having supper."I'll be right back." I said, excusing myself to the bathroom.

Me:

I'm glad you like it. I miss you. I can't wait to see you again, either.

Jasper:

Maggie does know about us now. I hope you aren't upset with me for telling her. I had to let her know why I never came in either. Believe it or not, she seemed really happy for us. I also promised her I would help her cover the phone lines while you're gone. Take as long as you need and please tell your mom and Abby I'm sorry I had to leave early. Good night, Angel. Though he did answer my question from earlier that day, I couldn't help but feel like I was subtly being dismissed. *Stop it, Carla! Don't overthink it!* I quickly told myself before typing out my reply.

Me:

Night, Jasper. Thanks for everything. Xo

Jasper:

Don't mention it. It's my pleasure. Xo

Chapter 15

⁓◌◍◌⁓

A
fter watching about half a dozen episodes of Hoarders with Mama, I was finally able to convince her to donate some of Joel's old clothes and tools. Over the next few days, I spent most of my time helping Mama dispose of things she really needed to let go of. We both knew that Joel would much rather hand them down to someone who could use them instead of sitting in her closet getting old and rusty only to collect dust. We settled on keeping a few of her favorite flannels and sweaters to reinvent them into a patch quilt she could tastefully display on her bed. Mama loved that idea!

We stumbled across our family photo albums when Mama dug out her old sewing machine. I always enjoyed reminiscing through old family photos. Looking back, it was clear to me that I had major Daddy issues while growing up as I recalled the spiritual connection I kept within my daily thoughts. The positive impact Joel's presence in our lives was pointedly evident in the photos that were strewn across Mama's full sized bed. I was quite surprised by how genuinely happy I appeared as a teenager. It was hard not to notice the flicker of light that danced in my eyes in each of the photos I had taken presence in.

As I peered deep into the evidence of a life I had, before I met AJ, it seemed funny to me that one bad relationship could bring me to the darkness I felt inside when I lived in Wakefield. How the light in my eyes had been left behind, somewhere within the distant memories of these albums. To the outside world, you'd never know it behind the mask of a smile I always wore. Like an eclipse, the darkness within his heart had somehow consumed the light in mine.

For now, I could only be grateful to have been drawn away from him. Away from the dark, and into the light. A place where life seemed to meet avenues of opportunity rather than dead ends. Where friendships were able to bloom, where they once seemed to whither away. And romance blossomed after a single taste of Jasper's lips. I knew I was hooked. My head knew it, my soul knew it, it was my heart that was still somewhat torn. I had been left with a sense of hesitation after the sting of AJ's darkness that had spawn into my life. AJ broke my heart into a thousand pieces and shattered my soul, I was sure of that! It wasn't that my heart was not repairable… that was clear with every comforting beam of surprise that came from being in the company of Jasper's presence. I truly felt the repair of every shattered piece of my soul in his nurturing touch.

Each and every morning, I woke up to a "Good morning" text message from Jasper. We spoke briefly on the phone late in the evening on Thursday night. It was just after Abby's new boyfriend, Chase, left from having dinner with us. I was delighted at the chance to get to meet him. Watching the two of them together honestly made my spirit dance with joy. They were both clearly smitten with one another. I was so happy for Abby to have found someone kind and caring at such a young age. Not to say they would last forever as they were both only sixteen. It was still comforting to know she wouldn't face the sort of relationship like the one I had with AJ if she and Chase were together.

Chase made a great first impression when he brought us chocolate chip cookies to have for dessert. He baked them fresh, himself. They were only the slice and bake kind by Pillsbury, but the gesture was sweet and far from being lost on Mama and me. Neither were the tasty cookies.

I could still feel Jasper's interest in me sprinkled throughout our text message conversations, but his heart still seemed a little lost in the mist. There were no words spoken between us that would have led me to believe that there were any major concerns to worry about within our relationship, it was more of a sense that I felt from a lack in his energy towards me. I couldn't quite put my finger on it, but there was definitely something missing.

It wasn't until the phone call that I received on Friday morning from Jamie that left me feeling deeply concerned about everything I knew of our relationship. She called me in between her first 2 classes because she thought it was important information I should have about Jasper. Apparently, she had been sitting in her car, about to leave for school, when she saw Jasper walk out of the lobby with some bleach blonde girl around our age.

My heart sank the moment Jamie described her to me. I had no doubt it was the same girl from the club. It had to be! Her description matched perfectly. Petite, shoulder length blonde hair. "They were fighting with each other." Jamie said through the phone. "I ducked down in my seat as soon as I saw them come outside, but I was too far away to hear what they were saying. I don't want to worry you, but I do think you should know what I saw, at the very least." Jamie said with a tinge of guilt in her voice. It was clear that she was afraid of how I might take the news.

"No, it's fine," I said with a swallow of the lump that seemed to magically appear in my throat. "I'm glad you told me. He has been distant since he left. I wonder what they could have been arguing about." I paused for a moment to picture the scene Jamie described and my mind was quick to draw the worst possible conclusion. "Do you think he's seeing her on the side?" Even though Jasper may have openly staked his claim on me, we technically hadn't had the discussion of being exclusive.

"I honestly couldn't tell you. What I can say is that whatever they were arguing about must have been serious. Jasper looked so pissed!"

"Okay, well I don't want to keep you, I know you have to get to class. I appreciate you letting me know. I guess I'll have to decide on whether I should bring it up to him or not," I said.

"I'm sorry, honey. I wish it were better news. I'll keep you posted if anything else comes to light. Love you, Babes," Jamie said.

"Yes! Please do. Love you too!" I replied before ending the call.

~

As the day pressed on, I tried my best to keep myself busy. I ran errands to help Mama out and brought the box of Joel's tools and clothes for donation down to the local Good Will. No matter how hard I tried, I still couldn't seem to keep the image of Jasper and that blonde bimbo from the club from resurfacing into my mind.

It irked me to no end, not knowing what they could have been arguing about. And although I was really beginning to form an attachment to the attention Jasper had shown me, along with the butterfly sensations that brushed my core each and every time he set his eyes in my direction, I still felt as though I had no right to demand him to tell me what was going on between them.

We never labeled ourselves as official. Sure, every action he took towards me stated otherwise, but without the words spoken between us officially, I honestly couldn't say he was off the market in the dating pool.

I walked through the day caught somewhere between a state of restlessness and hopelessness. So much that I hadn't even appreciated the nostalgia of being back home, traveling down all the old familiar roads.

With so many miles between Jasper and me, I was far from within reach of his touch to soothe me. Without his reassuring presence filling me with praise and nurturing my soul as he always seemed to do, I was eager to find a way to calm my mind. My only solution was the bright idea to hang out with my old friends, Heather and Amber. At the very least, it might entertain me enough to help take my mind off all of these things I had no control over.

I pulled my phone out of my pocket in search of Amber's number and dialed it since it was too early to call Heather. She didn't get off of work until later that afternoon. After a few rings, Amber picked up the line.

"Oh my God... Happy Birthday!" She sang through the phone. "I'm so sorry, I forgot to call you! How've you been?"

I laughed. "Don't worry… it's totally fine. I actually called to let you know that I'm actually here in town." I replied.

"You are?!" She cried.

"Yes! I am. What are you guys doing tonight?" I quickly asked.

"We're having poker night… You should totally come! Tommy's invited a couple of his friends and it'll just be Heather and me, we can definitely use another player!" I couldn't lie, the invitation did sound enticing. It had been so long since I played. We used to host poker parties twice a month when Heather, Amber and I lived together. We typically played tournament style for $20 per person. Winner takes all, or split between the final 2 players. I had my share of wins and was curious to know if I still had it in me.

"I don't see why not? Sure. 8 o'clock as usual?" I asked.

"Yes, same as always. Unless you wanna come by a little early to help us set up. It's been ages since we had your famous spinach dip! Can you make it?" *Ahh!* This was exactly the distraction I needed. Something else to focus my energy on, rather than any potential threat to the relationship between Jasper and me.

"OK, I'm sure Mama and Abby will be happy to have their living room back for a night," I laughed. "I will stop by the market on the way to grab what I need. Do you guys need anything else?" I asked.

"Not unless you find something else you'd want while you're there,

I'm pretty sure we have everything else covered." She said, "Heather made watermelon and green apple jello shots last night and Tommy's stopping to buy beer on his way home." She added.

"Okay, I guess I will see you guys later then." I said.

"Okay, sounds good! Can't wait to see you!" Amber cried.

"Me either! See you guys soon!" I said before ending the call with Amber.

Chapter 16

It was all fun and games. Right up until things got a bit out of hand at Heather and Amber's place. At first, it was nice to catch up with my old roommates. As soon as the festivities began, I caved and partook in the seemingly harmless jello shots. I was 4 shots and 2 beers in by the time I lost my $20 entry fee for being the first one in the poker tournament to make it into the loser's lounge. My stack had been dwindling down as the antes were raised and I went all in with pocket queens only to be met with a flush of diamonds to my opponent on the river.

I secretly wondered if it was Tommy's intention to get me alone, when he sat down next to me on the couch in the living room after tapping out of the tournament a few minutes later. It wasn't until I had succumbed to a drunken kiss from Tommy's lips that I quickly lost my own self respect. This kiss was not at all how I had previously imagined it would be. Back when I would daydream about having the chance. The guilt instantly flooded in, like the storm surge of a hurricane. I was quick to withdraw from his embrace.

With Jasper, everything inside me felt raw, unhinged and full of passion when we kissed. Whereas, with Tommy, it felt more like kissing my brother, if I ever had one. The distinction of the two quickly sobered me to the fact that I had foolishly let my guard down and betrayed whatever bond Jasper and I had in a matter of seconds.

After that, I felt so sick to my stomach that I felt the need to leave the party. Thankfully it was only a few blocks away from Mama's house and I could easily just walk back to her apartment.

Heather and Amber were both too drunk and deeply engaged in the poker tournament with Tommy's friends to even notice that I was leaving. Despite my resistance, Tommy, refused to let me walk home by myself. I agreed when he told me he only wanted to make sure I got home okay. My attraction to him was clearly not the type I was looking for in a romantic relationship where I had once thought it was, but I still respected him as a friend and was truly grateful that he cared enough to see me home.

It was late when I got inside Mama's apartment. Mama and Abby had both retreated to their rooms for the night, so it was just me and the couch. I turned on the TV for some background noise as I plopped myself down and reflected on just how much I seemed to have outgrown my life, as it was, here in Virginia.

I was honestly surprised at how quickly my heart had made its home in Boston with Jamie and my new friends. Oh, and let's not forget, Jasper and Lucas! My only question was, did I have Jasper's whole heart? Or was I sharing him with someone else? I couldn't help but to lay there pondering on the very thought I had been trying to escape all day as I drifted off to sleep.

Chapter 17

W hen the sunlight flashed her laser beams over my eyelids through the blinds of Mama's living room window, I squeezed my eyes shut and buried my head into the cushions of the couch. I could hear Abby rummaging through the kitchen cabinets. Every morsel of cereal that hit Abby's bowl sounded as if they had been blasted into my ears though soundproof headphones. My head was pounding like the drum on the back of the energizer bunny.

"Morning, sunshine." Abby said with a cocky smirk spread across her mouth. Yes, I heard it without even seeing it. "You *are* coming with us today, right?" She asked. We had plans to go to the mall to find her dress for the homecoming dance. I had been looking forward to it all week. I just wish I didn't wake up feeling like I had been hit by a semi truck. I groaned into the couch before I could bring my voice to the surface for a reply.

"What time is it?" I asked.

"It's 10:15," She said with a crunchy bite of her cereal as she stood over me.

I sighed. "Yes, I'm coming. I just need to sleep a little while longer."

"Where's your car? I didn't see it out in the parking lot when I took Crystal for a walk this morning," She asked with an unwelcoming reminder that I needed to go pick it up from Heather and Amber's apartment this morning. I lay there wondering if I could somehow do it without being noticed. By now, I was sure that everyone knew that Tommy kissed me. A mess I had no interest in cleaning up, at least not on a morning like this.

"It's at Amber's house. I was too drunk to drive last night, so Tommy walked me home." I said, realizing that there was no time to sleep off my headache. I opened my eyes just in time to catch the side eye Abby shot me.

"Tommy? The guy you were crushing on for years?! *He* walked you home? What about Jasper?" She asked, kicking me in the gut with my reality. It was far too much for me to even consider thinking about, especially with this nagging hangover.

"Water. Advil. Please?" I asked, kindly letting her know that last night's festivities were currently off the table for discussion.

"What time are we leaving?" I asked, bringing my feet from off the couch onto the carpeted floor in a half-ass attempt to sit up. Abby set the glass of water and bottle of Advil I had asked her for on the coffee table and sat down next to me on the couch as she continued to chomp away at her cereal. "Not until 1 o'clock. Mama had to take a client out to run some shopping errands this morning." Mama's odd hours as a living nurse aid was nothing new to me. Ever since Joel's passing, she took advantage of every opportunity she had to work in order to keep up with the bills on her own.

After several tries at opening the pill bottle, I pushed the Advil in Abby's direction. She opened it and handed me a few to take before proceeding with her crunching. I drank half the glass of water with them and set it back down on the coffee table.

"Hey squirt… Why don't you do your big sis a solid and go pick up my car from Heather and Amber's place for me while I sleep off this headache?" I figured she would jump at the chance to drive my car since she had just gotten her license a few months ago. I had yet to see her driving in action, but I knew it was only a few blocks away. I was hoping I could trust her driving skills enough to make it across a few streets on her own without supervision.

"Heck yeah!" She cried, clearly excited for the opportunity.

"Come straight back here, please. I'm going to try to get some rest, so don't wake me when you get back please." I said, producing the keys from the back pocket of the jeans I was still wearing from the night before.

"I will, I promise!" She said. "I'll go get dressed!" She cried as she leapt up off the couch. In her departure, I let myself sink back into the soft cushions of Mama's couch and closed my eyes.

Morning fog surrounded me as I followed the path to an old house where Jasper was standing on the front porch waving me over. I finally made my way to the top of the hill the house stood on only to find that he'd already gone inside.

The front door was cracked open. As I entered, the creek of the floorboards startled me and the house had completely morphed itself into one of those fun houses you see at the fair. I was completely surrounded by mirrors. I gasped when I saw that the reflection staring back at me was tainted with filth. There was dirt splattered across my face, from what I could see in the dust filled air.

I tried to run, but the mirrors were everywhere. I couldn't seem to find my way to Jasper who was calling out to me from somewhere off in the distance. For a moment, I was able to catch a glimpse of him in one of the mirrors, but before I could make my way near, his reflection disappeared.

I was lost, with only one clear message from my dirty reflection staring back at me. The words "Come clean" slowly emerged onto the foggy mirror. I didn't quite understand it at first, but the moment it dawned on me, the dust settled and the mirrors had all vanished into thin air, taking my dirty reflection along with it.

Jasper was standing over by the window in the corner of the room. His arms were outstretched towards me with light cascading in from the sun that was shining in through the window, behind him. I needed to come clean.... I was only a few steps away from him, when I cried out, "I have to tell him!"

"Tell who? What?" Abby asked, as she shook me awake.

My eyes fluttered open at the sound of her voice, the dream eluded itself back into my subconscious for the time being.

"What?" I asked.

"You were just talking in your sleep. I know you told me not to wake you, but…" She started to say.

"What time is it?" I asked.

Abby looked down at her watch. "It's quarter to twelve. Mama will be here soon. We should start getting ready."

"Right, uh…" I gathered my thoughts. My headache had subsided, *Thank God!* I got up from the couch and headed for the bathroom in a hurry. "I need to grab a shower real quick. Can you put on a pot of coffee for me, please?" I asked, as I walked past her in pursuit of the only bathroom in Mama's small apartment.

"I guess!" Abby huffed. "Your keys are on the hook by the door, by the way."

"Thanks, squirt! I appreciate you doing that for me!" I called out before closing the bathroom door behind me.

"Anytime!" She called back.

Chapter 18

After storming nearly every rack from 3 different department stores inside the mall, Abby finally settled on a dress for her Homecoming Dance. Even then, she seemed as though she weren't completely sold.

"It's perfect! You look beautiful!" Mama said. A perfect shade of deep fuchsia to complement the golden locks of Abby's hair. The dress she had on was heart-shaped on top and hugged her at the waist with just the right sway in the skirt to bring whatever dance moves she had to that next level. I could honestly cry at how stunning she looked. My sister had always been a bit of a tomboy. The opportunity alone, to see her in a dress, had already brought me to tears.

"I agree... They all look beautiful on you if you ask me." Leila chimed, as she twirled around in front of the mirror while dangling a matching sheer sash to her own long and flowing, daffodil colored gown. Her dress had a side split clean up to her mid-thigh. By this time, I was feeling very thankful that Kallie had already decided on her own turquoise sequin dress 2 stores ago. My stomach was growling at me like a mad cat! I needed to eat before it swallowed me whole.

"You both look stunning! Now, Let's go eat!" I said, swiping a tear away from off my cheek. Mama just laughed. She knew how irritated I got whenever I was hangry. The lingering remnants of my hangover was of no help, either.

"I really love this sash that comes with it, I think I'm sold. What do you think, Abby?" Leila asked.

"You look beautiful." Abby replied. "I'm hungry, too! Let's just buy them and go have lunch." *Praise the Lord!*

Mama, Kallie and I all gathered the tags for the dresses and headed up to the cashier counter, while Abby and Leila removed the dresses they were trying on and got dressed in the clothes that they were initially wearing.

After paying for the dresses, we all exited the store and walked through the mall in pursuit of the food court for lunch. Many center aisle vendors approached us with their perfumes, lotions and cosmetics. Any other time, I would have stopped to smell them and try them all out myself, but I was on a mission to feed this nasty beast of hunger inside me. So much that I literally had to tear Leila away from one of the vendors.

Naturally, I was the first to sit at the table with my tray of food and I was in no mood to wait for anyone. Pizza was typically 'my go to' at the mall, but I added a sushi roll because I was starving. It was in no way near as fresh as the sushi I had up in Boston at the Thai place that Jamie and I gone to in celebration of my first job at the coffee shop.

It did, however, serve its purpose in filling my belly and settled my nerves from being so hungry. I was about to take a bite of my pizza when my phone buzzed in my pocket.

Jasper

Hey you... How are things going? Will you be coming back soon? I miss you.

The fact that he was missing me sent the idea of whatever may or may not have been going on with the blonde bimbo to the wayside. All I needed to hear was that he wanted me there, where he was. In a sudden flash, my dream whipped back into my conscience, hitting me like a ton of bricks. The message "Come Clean" was playing over and over like some old broken record in my mind. I just knew I couldn't keep the fact that I had kissed Tommy a secret between us. I *had* to tell him. The only question... Was I brave enough to tell him in person, or would I be better off sending it in a text? Before I could even give my conscience a chance to lose my nerve, my fingers had a mind of their own. I quickly pushed the reply button on my phone and began typing out my response.

Me:

I need to tell you something.

Jasper:

I'm all ears, Angel.

Me:

I kissed someone last night, I didn't mean to. Well, technically he kissed me and I take full responsibility for kissing him back, but it wasn't you... I was drunk and just not thinking straight. It felt very wrong. And... well, I'm sorry, but I just couldn't keep it to myself. I had to tell you. My text was met with the longest five minutes of silence in my entire life. And when I could no longer take it, what else could I do but ramble on some more?

Me:

I was confused. Ever since you left for Boston, you've been distant and we never really discussed our exclusivity. I'm so sorry. Please don't be angry with me.

Jasper:

Just come home. Please? I'm not mad, just hurt. I've had a rough week and I just really need you here. We can talk about it when you get back. By this time, all the girls and Mama had all joined me at the table with their own trays of food. I didn't want to be rude, so I sent him a quick reply back.

Me:

Okay. I just have to tell Mama and Abby. I'll try to head out tomorrow morning.

In all reality, I still hadn't heard anything back from Ben. I could only imagine that by now, he must have been furious with me. Despite whatever avenues it took to get back within his good graces, I really wanted to keep my job at the coffee shop. I just knew that if I had stayed here any longer, he was sure to hire someone else. Besides, Abby seemed to be taking things well enough. In fact, I wouldn't be surprised if it even phased her at all, at this point. She and I were very different in that way when it came to our emotions. I tended to bottle things up, where she had always been very forthcoming when something was bothering her. The whole town knew when Abby was upset!

"Aren't you going to eat?" Mama asked me, bringing to light the fact that my pizza was getting cold. *YUCK!* Everyone else was finished eating. The girls were all chatting away about their dresses and whether their dates would like them.

"Yes. sorry. That was Jasper who texted me." I said, as I took a bite of my pizza.

"Don't be sorry, honey, you were the one who was starving. Is everything okay in Boston?" She asked.

"Actually, I do need to get back if I want to keep my jobs. I just need to talk to Jamie, just to be sure she's okay with me coming back."

"Well, I would hate to see you leave, but I know my apartment is too small for you to be shacking up on the couch. It sounds to me like you were really making your way up there. I could never ask you to stay. Perhaps Abby and I could come visit *you* sometime."

"Are you leaving me, already?! You just got back!" Abby asked, bringing a quick halt to the conversation she was in with her friends. Clearly, she was upset to learn that I was leaving.

"Yes, I'm leaving for Boston tomorrow morning. I wish I could stay with you guys a little longer, but I have to get back if I want to have any chance at keeping my new jobs."

"I guess you're right. Plus, I'm sure you wouldn't want to keep a hottie like Jasper waiting around for too long anyway or he may find someone else. You guys should see my sister's new boyfriend!" She said, quickly turning her attention back to her friends.

Well, that went much smoother than I thought it would. The Abby I knew would have easily thrown a tantrum and begged me to stay. My little squirt was really growing up! I had to admit, Abby's words did sting a little but I knew she had no way of knowing anything about the conversation I had with Jamie yesterday about the blond bimbo from the club. I really couldn't blame her for being insensitive to something she had no knowledge on.

"Hey, do you mind if we make a stop over at the Pop's Corn stand? I want to bring some kettle corn back with me to Boston for Jamie." I asked Mama.

"Of course, Honey. I'm sure she'd love that!"

That night, I called Jamie to let her know that I would be making my way back in the morning just to make sure she was still okay with me staying with her. Why I would even have any doubt is beyond me! I could literally hear her jumping up and down in excitement!

"Oh, Good! So you don't mind?" I asked.

"Stop it! You know this place is way too quiet without you here. Don't get me wrong, I do love having my own apartment but having my BFF here with me is like the icing on the cake!" She replied.

"Awesome! I miss you too! I'll see you tomorrow, then!" I said.

"Drive safe, I'll see you soon!" She said before ending the call.

Chapter 19

The next day, Mama got herself up at 4 am to cook me breakfast. She knew I was planning on leaving before dawn for my seven hour trip to Boston. It had been ages since I had Mama's famous cheese grits and eggs. I swear she added a touch of magic! No matter how I ever tried, I could never get mine to taste anywhere near as good as hers. It was funny, because Mama wasn't much of a cook. Joel and I used to take turns cooking most of our family dinners before he passed. There were a few signature dishes Mama made, however, that just hit in all the right spots. Her cheese Grits and eggs were one of those dishes.

"I'm really gonna miss you Mama." I said, before heading out the door with 3 extra large bags of gourmet popcorn tucked under my arm and a large trash bag full of clothes I had taken the time to launder the night before.

"We're gonna miss you too!" She said, giving me a squeeze. I was surprised to see Abby peek her head out through her bedroom door. "Wait! Don't leave!" She cried out as she quickly slammed the door closed behind her and made a dash for the kitchen where Mama and I were standing.

"Okay," I replied, "I'm just gonna load this stuff in the car real quick!" I said as I proceeded through the front door. Abby appeared just as I was closing the trunk to my car.

"I'm surprised you're up this early, squirt!" I said, giving her bed head a tousle.

"I couldn't just let you leave without saying Good-bye! Thanks for coming to 'rescue' me!" she laughed. The fact that she could joke about the whole thing eased me out of any lingering guilt I may have had about going back to Boston.

"You know I could never live with myself if anything had ever happened to you, squirt. I hope you and Mama will come to visit me sometime, soon."

Mama appeared at my car door just in time for a long and sappy Good-bye scene you would typically see in Hallmark movies. She handed me one of Joel's old lunch coolers full of drinks and snacks. "Please make sure you eat and stay hydrated." She said as she pulled me in for a hug that would last longer than a full minute. "Love you honey. Please, don't be a stranger."

"Thanks, Mama! I love you too! I'll let you know when I get there." I said as I got in my car and drove off. I watched through the window as they both waved their good-byes to me. I waved back and hit the road.

Chapter 20

My drive back to Boston was moving rather smoothly with Sunday traffic. The open road gave me a good amount of time to reflect on the past week's events. I did stop for gas a few times and twice to use the restroom since Mama packed enough food and drinks for a 3 day trip in the lunch box she sent with me.

I arrived at Jamie's apartment building just before 1 o'clock. I had quite a bit to bring upstairs with me, so I went inside to borrow one of the dolly carts I had seen the elderly tenants use for their groceries from time to time.

I was surprised to see Charlie, the security guard, on a Sunday. It was typically his day off. He greeted me with a great big smile. "Miss Carla, I was worried about you! How are you, dear?" He asked.

"I'm doing fine, Charlie. It's good to see you… What are you doing here on a Sunday?" I asked.

"Benson took the weekend off to attend his daughter's wedding. I had nothing better to do today, so I took over his shift. What about you? What had you running out of here so quickly the other day?" He asked, curiosity swirling behind his glasses.

"Oh... I had a family emergency and had to go back to Virginia for a bit. I'm so sorry I didn't say Good-bye. I was in a big hurry, I didn't mean to be rude."

"Don't you worry about that, I'm just happy to see that you're back. There haven't been any mysterious packages for you while you were gone." He said with a wink. I could feel my cheeks warming at the mere mention of Jasper's gifts. I honestly couldn't wait to see him later, so that we could hopefully put everything behind us.

I laughed. "Good to know, thanks!" I winked back. "Well, Charlie... I'd better be off. It's been a long drive back and I can really use a nap! It's been nice chatting with you," I said with a smile.

"Likewise, my dear." He smiled back.

When I wheeled the dolly cart inside the front door of Jamie's apartment, I had fully expected to see Jamie, sitting on the couch watching TV, like she always did on Sundays. What I didn't expect to see was Dillon sitting there with her in his boxer shorts. He quickly grabbed a pillow to cover himself when he saw me walk through the door.

"Oh, you're back!" Jamie couldn't seem to hold back her chuckle at Dillon's quick reflexes. Clearly, he felt awkward to have been caught without his clothes on.

"I'm so sorry" I said, quickly turning my head in the other direction. "I hope I'm not... interrupting anything. Pay no mind to me!" I said as I awkwardly wheeled the dolly cart back to my bedroom, making sure to keep my eyes away from their direction.

"It's fine!" Jamie quickly hopped off the couch to come and help me with my bags, while Dillon scurried off to Jamie's bedroom to hide from his embarrassment. "I just didn't think you would be back so early. Dillon surprised me and came down to see me last night." Jamie said, with an ear to ear smile spread across her face.

"You got lucky last night, didn't you?" I shouted in a whisper as I closed my bedroom door behind us.

"A good girl never kisses and tells... Who am I kidding, I think we both know I'm not a good girl! Yes, we did it..." She cried. "And yes, it was amazing!" Jamie closed her eyes to briefly indulge in her memory of the night before. "Let's just say, all of those yoga classes I've been waking up so early for have really come in handy." She said with a mischievous raise of her eyebrows.

"OMG! You did, didn't you!" I said excitedly, still trying to keep my voice out of Dillon's earshot. I doubted he could hear me with 2 closed doors between us, but I didn't want to embarrass him any further. "No wonder why you're glowing," I said as I struggled to pry my suitcase open. "Well, I'm happy to hear that you finally you got some!" I said, sighing at my inability to open the zipper. I had my heart set on unpacking before my nap, but with all the trouble it was giving me, I was ready to give up on it for the time being. "I left early this morning so I could come back and get some rest before I talk to Jasper. Have you seen or heard anything else I should know about?" I asked, curiously.

"No, that was the only time I saw her. I wonder what they were arguing about." She replied.

"You and me, both! I really don't want to ask him about it though... I don't know why, but my instincts are telling me to let him open up when he's ready to. Whenever I'm with him, I just feel so safe. Like I can trust him, ya know? It's really strange because you know I don't easily trust very many people this early on," I said.

"Well, if you trust him, then so do I. You should have seen his reaction when you left. He was genuinely concerned. He's definitely crazy about you, I have no doubt about that! But I will definitely be keeping my eye out for sure and will let you know if anything else pops up!"Hearing Jamie's depiction of how Jasper reacted to me leaving did give me hope and eased some of the tension I had about seeing him later. But I needed to open up to her and see what she thought about what had happened between Tommy and me while I was gone. More in the matter of how I should handle things with Jasper. My heart was still with him, there was no question about that, because no matter how hard I tried, I just couldn't get him off my mind.

"Something else happened while I was back home. Do you remember Amber's brother, Tommy?" I asked.

"Vaguely, I think I only met him once or twice. That's the guy you were crushing on for a while before you met AJ, right? The one you found out had a girlfriend?" She asked.

"Yes! So... I went to Heather and Amber's to play poker and had a few too many drinks. Anyway, he kissed me and I kissed him back, and... well, let's just say that old crush died with the kiss." I laughed.

It just felt like I was kissing a relative or something. I didn't feel any spark whatsoever, not like the rush I get when Jasper kisses me."

"Well, that's certainly one way to tell, for sure! Are you going to tell Jasper about it?" Jamie asked. "I know you... You're conscience won't let you keep it from him for very long, I'm sure. I would just go ahead and get it out of the way." Jamie knew me well!

"I already did." I confessed. "We haven't really talked about it though. I'm assuming we will tonight."

"I wouldn't worry too much about it. You'll know soon enough. I'm telling you, he's crazy about you. He drove 7 hours to come find you. That alone should tell you where you stand with him. Speaking of kissing, I'd probably better get back to Dillon. You should have seen the "deer caught in headlights" look on his face when you walked through the door!" She laughed.

"I would have given you a heads up, had I known he was here." I said.

"Don't worry about it. He'll live beyond the embarrassment. I'm just happy that you're back! Want me to close the door?" She asked.

"Yes, please... I'm gonna lay down for a little bit." I replied as I let myself sink into the luxurious dressings of my new bed. Well, technically the bed belonged to Jamie's parents, but it was officially mine to use while they weren't here to visit. I took a few minutes to catch up on the text messages that came through on my drive back to Boston. I scrolled through my phone to find out who they were from.

Jasper:

Good morning, Angel. Hope you are on your way. Drive safe and please let me know when you get here.

Me:

Hey ;) I was driving. And yes, I just got in. I'm going to lay down for a little while, I'll call you later when I wake up.

Brooke:

Hey Girl! Are you coming back anytime soon? I think Ben is gonna blow a gasket if you're not here on Tuesday. 🐝

Me:

Just got back! Tell him to hold his knickers I'll be there Tuesday morning with bells and whistles! I have so much to tell you!

After sending out my replies, I set my phone to charge and closed my eyes to charge myself. I must have fallen asleep fast, because I didn't hear either message chime back from Jasper or Brooke.

Chapter 21

J amie and Dillon were headed out for dinner when I woke up. I wandered into the kitchen and made myself a cup of tea to bring outside with me. I sat on the balcony taking in the view of the sky, wildly dressed in pink and orange hues, as I quietly gathered my thoughts. The sunset was as beautiful as ever and the air had just enough chill in it to make me go back inside to grab a sweater. I picked my phone up from off the charger and took it with me. There were two missed text notifications. One was from Jasper and one was from Brooke. Both replying back to the texts I had sent them before I crashed out.

Brooke:

Can't wait to hear all about it!

Jasper:

I really need to see you... Come upstairs whenever you're ready

By this time, there had been 5 days of space and time between Jasper and me and 2 separate events happening within that time frame. Both occurrences held strong potential to divide us and 1 still remained a mystery to me. I had chosen to put my trust in Jasper, in hopes that he might open up to me about what happened with the girl from the club. Whether we were exclusive or not, we were still far too early in our relationship for me to feel entitled to know everything about him that he wasn't ready to share with me... At least not yet, anyway.

My heart felt for him because I knew he was going through something. The idea of pressuring him to open up to me was honestly the furthest thought from my mind. All I wanted right now was to bring him some comfort and maybe a little something else to take his mind off of whatever it was that had been ailing him all week. That's not to say that it didn't irk me, the mystery being left unsolved. What mattered more to me than anything else was that he could forgive me for my mishap with Tommy and that stupid, meaningless kiss. What I truly *needed* was reassurance that Jasper and I were going to be okay.

With all of this at stake, it became clear that I had been procrastinating the day away on something I would inevitably find out once I saw him face to face. It could only go 1 of 2 ways and I was in no way, shape or form, feeling secure about my odds of things going in my favor. All I could do was pray he might find it in his heart to forgive me so that we could have a chance of moving on from it.

The more I thought about it, the more my stomach twisted itself in knots. It was time to face whatever issues we had so I could finally move past it. With my nerves on edge I quickly launched out of my chair and went inside to shower and dress.

As the water cascaded over me, some of the most intimate moments Jasper and I shared with each other washed over my mind. I quietly relished in the sweet revival of my confidence in the steam of the hot shower as I recalled the way he looked at me. Most of the time, I felt unworthy of being one to catch Jasper's eye in the first place. I fully intended on chasing down whatever luck I had the day I met him and made a vow to pull out all the stops in regaining Jasper's attention.

I decided to wear the dress he bought me for my birthday, so he could finally see it on me in person. Though I didn't put on any makeup, I did invest some time in my skin care routine and sprayed a dab of perfume behind my ear and on my wrists. Soon I was out the door before my conscience had any time to open a window for doubt to settle in.

~

I pressed the button for the elevator and the pin code for Jasper's floor. When the door opened, my senses were enlightened by jazz music playing softly in the background and a dimly lit version of Jasper's penthouse. The only light I could see was shining in from above the kitchen stove and the flames of candles that appeared to be lit on every surface within my sight. What I couldn't see was any sign of Jasper or Lucas.

As my eyes began to adjust to the dim light of the candles, I was quickly awakened to Jasper's presence as he swept me into his arms from behind and pinned up me against the wall between the bookcase and his desk.

Before I could utter a single word, he turned my body around to face him and firmly pressed his lips on mine. Every emotion I had in me quickly rose to the surface as I fervently kissed him back. And this was no ordinary kiss. It was a kiss that held power to effortlessly take my breath away. I soon began to lose my balance from the surprise of the heady rush that crashed over me. Jasper quickly brought his hand to my waist to steady me. His other hand fell gracefully through my hair as he continued to unleash the fiery passion within himself into my more than eager lips. An intense electric feeling so indescribably surreal coursed through me. There was a distinct sense of urgency behind his desire that sparked me to wonder: *Did he need everything to be OK with us too? Was this his way of helping me to understand that I was not alone in how I was feeling?*

Jasper broke free from my lips to peer directly into my eyes. "Make no mistake, Angel. You are mine. And I am yours. Nothing will ever come between us." He whispered as his hands fell from my waist to give my ass a firm squeeze. He continued kissing me as if it were the only thing left in this world to soothe him.

The passion that had been rapidly intensifying between us was enough to make the earth shatter. It wouldn't even matter if it did because we were both exactly where we wanted to be, perfectly content within each other's grip.

Jasper quickly tossed a pile of magazines off his desk and onto the floor as if they mattered nothing. He lifted my body up off the ground and planted me in a seated position on top of his desk. I could still taste the wax from the candles he lit as he tantalizingly wedged his thumb inside my mouth. He quickly raced the tips of his fingers from his free hand up my inner thigh and under my dress where he soon discovered the silky texture of my thong. It must have pleased him well enough to invite that devilish grin of his to spread across his face. He stroked his fingers over the tiny stretch of fabric in a back and forth motion until I moaned.

Exploring my mouth with his thumb until he felt satisfied enough to withdraw, he quickly replaced his thumb with another passionate kiss from his mouth. "Every inch of you is mine, Angel." He groaned.

My body was quick to respond to his touch when he pulled my thong to the side and introduced his thumb, still wet from my saliva, to my newly exposed clitoris. He circled around until I could honestly take no more. "Jasper, please" I begged.

"All you ever have to do is ask, Angel...I will never deny you." He said, quickly shoving the chair away to lift me off the desk. He twirled me around and folded my body over to face forward against the surface. With the weight of my body resting on my hands and elbows, my eyes caught sight of the glass vase filled with freshly cut gardenias. *Ahh!* My senses were quickly addressed by the scent I had been trying to distinguish the moment I stepped inside Jasper's penthouse. A fragrance perfumed by paperback books and my favorite flowers.

My body quivered at the mere crinkling of the condom wrapper. I swear, he knew exactly what he was doing when he tore it open behind my ear with his teeth. By the time he pulled away from me to slide the condom on, I was already soaking wet, desperately longing for him to be inside me.

An all consuming rush of warm electric currents crashed over me, the moment he slipped inside. *Yes! This was exactly the reassurance I needed!*

With the weight of his body colliding into mine, I was brought to a place where I felt completely freed of my inhibitions. And when he tossed the auburn waves of my hair aside to kiss the soft flesh of skin on my neck behind my ear, I cried out in sweet pleasure. "Ahh..." *How was he so in tune with my body?* Sweet and vulnerable places I never even knew existed! Yet, here he was diving into each new territory, exploring every inch of me without a compass. He was taking full ownership of me in his possession.

He gingerly nibbled his way to my ear, whispering breaths of his own sweet pleasure while intensifying his grip on my hips. The sting of his fingers digging into my flesh was one that brought a perfect balance between pain and pleasure. Instinctively, my body responded as my pelvis rocked back against him in the motion of his rhythm.

"That's it, Angel. Can you feel how hard I am for you?" He asked.

"Yes!" I breathed back.

"This is what happens when you keep me waiting for you." He purred into my ear as he gracefully pulled me away from the desk and guided me over to the sofa. For a moment, I wondered just how long he'd been waiting for me as I cast my view upon the dripping candles that were strewn across the coffee table.

Jasper quickly retained my attention back to the moment we were in when he thrust inside me with a force to be reckoned with. "Eyes on me, Angel." He said in a throaty whisper. "I'm gonna make you come so hard, you won't dream of putting your lips on another guy again." Currently, we were splayed out on his soft white leather sofa, my back against the couch and him on top of me in a missionary style position.

My hands were tied down above my head under the weight of one of Jasper's hands. With his free hand, he gently tucked a stray hair away from my face and curtained it behind my ear so he could stare directly into my eyes. His gaze was so intense, I swear I could honestly feel my soul pool inside the ocean of his eyes.

He wriggled his fingers between my legs like a master set of keys to my box of treasure, turning each one in a series of thrushes. Crashing in and out of me like the waves of the ocean, Jasper had me shamelessly crying out in ecstasy. I was completely bared to him, holding nothing back! No matter how hard I tried to dull down my pleasure for fear of embarrassment, I could not escape this incredible spell he had me under.

It wasn't long after Jasper discovered my g-spot that my body completely took over and possessed my mind. I found my release in what truly felt like a euphoric gift from the divine. Jasper followed closely behind. My knees were shaking uncontrollably, my heart was pounding and my body shuttered from the orgasm Jasper had just delivered. I let my hands studiously wander up and down each ripple of muscle in Jasper's back, as we both lay wrapped in each other's arms on his couch, trying to steady our breaths.

After some time, Jasper peeked his head up from my chest to look at me. "I'm sorry for being distracted, I didn't mean to make you feel like you didn't have my undivided attention." Jasper said, breaking the silence between us. "Promise me you won't ever run away from me like that again, Angel. Regardless of what I have going on, I want you to know that you will always be my first priority."

I had everything I needed in Jasper's declaration. With his words, he softened the space for me to apologize. And yet somehow, by taking responsibility on his part of the equation, he removed my need to. It wasn't enough, however, to steer my conscience clear. I felt just as responsible. Not only for leaving him without a trace, but also for betraying his trust. Whether our relationship had been clearly defined at the time or not, the fact was, there was no longer any confusion of Jasper's initial intentions with me. And I needed now, was to hold myself accountable too. Especially if we were to gain a solid foundation for our new beginning.

"I'm sorry, too." I said. "I never meant to hurt you, I just didn't know what else to do..."

Jasper quickly put his finger over my mouth. "Shh... It's OK, Angel. I'm just happy you are safe and that you are here with me," He said. He strengthened the grip of his hold around me as we lay there in his candle-lit apartment. It felt as though the rest of the world had disappeared. There was only us, as we relished in the tranquil waters of our emotional confessions. Right up until our peaceful silence was broken by Lucas and his cries from the loft upstairs.

"I guess someone's up from his nap." Jasper sighed. "I should probably take him out."

"That's probably a good idea," I agreed with a laugh.

Jasper went upstairs to let Lucas out of his crate. I stood to straighten myself up a bit. Within minutes, I was batting Lucas down from towering over me with kisses.

"Lucas! Down, Boy!" Jasper called as he came barreling down the spiral staircase after Lucas holding his leash. "I'm gonna take him out real quick. Are you hungry? Have you eaten?"

"Famished!" I said, admittedly.

"Do you like Greek food?" He asked. "I know a great place nearby we can easily walk to."

"I don't think I've ever Greek food before. Is it any good?" I asked.

"You'll love it!" He said, when he finally wrangled a hold on Lucas to put his leash on.

"Okay, that sounds good." I said, excited to see what he had in store for us. "Would you mind if I grab a quick shower while you're gone?" Thankfully, I had showered before coming up, but I felt sticky and sweaty from our surprise make up session.

"You don't ever have to ask, Angel…. Please, make yourself at home. We'll be back soon." He replied as he corralled Lucas into the elevator with him.

Chapter 22

I emerged from Jasper's guest bathroom to find 2 giant puppy dog eyes staring up at me and a little nub of a tail wagging like it had a mind of its own.

"Where's your daddy?" I asked Lucas, with a pat to his giant head as I found a cozy spot on the sofa next to him. I certainly wasn't expecting a response from a dog, but he did let out a cute little whimper when I mentioned the name, "Daddy". I assumed that Jasper had gone upstairs to get ready, so I waited patiently on the couch, while Lucas made a meal out of nibbling at my fingers.

A few minutes later, Jasper came down wearing a dark gray button up shirt and white denim jeans that hugged him in all the right places. Whatever cologne he was wearing, I was sure to follow, no matter where it might have led me. Delicious notes of leather and spice, with a cool freshly showered scent to finish. The emanating scent from his presence was intoxicating and sure to have me arrested for lusting after him without a conscience permit.

"Are you ready, beautiful?" He asked, alluring the butterflies in my belly to reawaken.

"Yes! Let's go!" I cried before I let on how easily his charming words affected my psyche. Jasper took my hand in his and pressed the button for the elevator. "It's a beautiful night. I really think you're gonna like the place we're going," He said, as he waved me into the elevator before him.

"I'm sure I will. You're an amazing cook, so I'm pretty sure I can trust your palette taste in food." I said, reassuringly.

"Mr. Sullivan," The security guard nodded in our direction. "Going out for another stroll?" He asked as we exited the elevator and entered the lobby. I hadn't seen this guy before. He was an older gentleman with a darker complexion. His name was Freddie, according to his name tag.

"It is a beautiful night and I have great company... What more can a guy ask for?" Jasper replied to the gentleman as he opened the door for me.

"You sure are a lucky fella!" Freddie agreed.

We stepped outside to find a bright full moon had risen to the sky among shades of a plum and violet painted dusk. A light breeze carried with it an air of romance as we were greeted with smiles from the people who passed us by. If you listened closely, you could hear the chiming of the Cathedral bells singing out from somewhere off in the distance.

"It's not too far, just a few blocks down." Jasper said, placing his hand in mine as we walked together down the paved sidewalk adjacent to the cobblestone street before us.

"I don't mind the walk at all, it's so pretty out tonight." I said, feeling grateful I was an avid fan of sneakers. "Do you ever go to church?" We had never discussed it before, but I was genuinely curious to know if Jasper was religious.

"I used to go with my friend, Sam and his mom when I was a teenager. To be honest, I haven't been to service in a while, but I do volunteer at the soup kitchen every now and then."

"That's so cool. I always wanted to do that." I said recalling my deep rooted desire to serve those who were less fortunate. I had always hoped to show them that there were people in this world who really do care. And perhaps remind them that there was beauty in where they were, as the only way from there would be up.

"How about you? Do you have a church that you go to?" Jasper asked, curiously.

"We used to go on Sundays as a family, when I was younger. We stopped going when my step daddy, Joel, passed away. I think it was just too painful for Mama." I replied.

"I can see how that would make sense. I'd love to take you to volunteer, sometime, if you'd like."

"I would honestly love that!" I agreed, genuinely excited for the chance.

"That sounds great… How about next Sunday?" He asked.

"Sounds like a date to me!" I replied as we turned the corner to find a row of various shops and restaurants. Some of the storefronts had mannequins dressed in fancy clothes. Others had windows that were lined with fresh baked breads and pastries. There was even one that was filled with decadent chocolates and candy apples just waiting to lure the nearest sweet tooth to its entrance.

"Well, we're here." Jasper said, as we approached the hostess stand at Helen's House.

"How many in your party?" The hostess asked.

"Table for 2 please, preferably a booth in the back if it's available." Jasper replied.

"I can arrange that for you, please follow me." She said as she crossed out a spot on the floor plan in front of her with a charcoal pen. She welcomed us inside to the tune of delightful micro tonal sounds of a guitar playing in the background that quickly set the stage for a truly romantic experience.

Cemented walls stood in contrast to the brick archways in the restaurant's charming decor. Vibrant paintings easily caught my attention to the old world kitchen utensils that hung from the walls. There were statues of Greek Gods found at each corner with vines of fragrant flowers wrapped all around them.

"Right this way." The hostess said as she guided us to a wrap-around booth set in the back of the restaurant. Adorned with bright blue fabric napkins, crystal wine glasses and antique silverware settings, the table was topped with a gorgeous floating candle for a centerpiece. With the refinement of its decor, it was clear the restaurant would definitely own a five star status on Trip Advisor and probably cost a pretty penny to eat at.

"Thank you," Jasper said to the hostess. He waited for me to make my way inside, then sat down next to me in the center of the booth.

"Can I offer you a wine menu?" She asked, blushing. It was clear, the hostess found Jasper attractive by the way her voice cracked. *Could I honestly blame her?*

"Yes, please." Jasper replied, pulling me closer to his side.

"Which would you prefer, Angel? Red or white?" Jasper asked me. He paid no attention to the hostess, who was clearly flustered by Jasper's presence, while I tried my best not to look at the prices on the menu before giving him my answer.

"Red, please. Do they have Sangria?" I asked.

"I'm sorry hon, we sure don't."

Jasper reached behind for his wallet. He handed the hostess a hundred dollar bill and took a quick glance at the menu. "Can you please ask the bartender for 2 wine glasses filled with ice and fruit and we'll take a bottle of Taurasi, please."

"Of course, sir." The hostess said as she quickly made her exit.

A few minutes later, we were greeted by our waiter with a tray of everything Jasper had requested, including a third glass that was empty. The waiter made a performance out of opening the bottle, and poured a small amount of wine into the empty glass as he handed it to Jasper to taste. He quickly placed the cork next to the bottle and waited for Jasper's nod of approval before proceeding to pour the wine into the glasses filled with fruit.

"May I present you with our specials?" The waiter asked.

"That won't be necessary. We'll have A tour of Greece for two please and an appetizer of Spanakopita," Jasper said as he handed the waiter our menus.

"An excellent choice, sir," The waiter was smiling, clearly happy with Jasper's selection.

"What's a Span-a-kopita?" I asked curiously when the waiter left our table. Jasper laughed at my struggle to pronounce the word. "If you like spinach, you'll love it! It's basically a puff pastry filled with spinach, feta cheese and Greek herbs."

"Oh, that sounds nice. I actually love spinach. Did I tell you, I make a killer spinach dip? Well, at least my old roommates, Amber and Heather think so. It's one of my favorite dishes that I make." I quickly humbled myself as I bit down on my lower lip. I couldn't help but wonder why I still felt so nervous being in close proximity to Jasper. After all, he was just inside me less than an hour ago. I couldn't seem to my finger on it, but he had this magical way of making me feel like I was in this constant dreamy state of walking among the clouds.

"You're adorable when you squirm, Angel. Makes me want to pull you under the table to 'settle' your nerves," He said in a sexy whisper. "I honestly can't wait to be the judge of this famous spinach dip of yours." He added with his notorious smirk. The one that showcased that lonely dimple from his left cheek. All while slithering his hand up my thigh. *Good God! What was he doing to me?!* I wondered as I batted down the butterflies from rising within my tummy.

"We're in a restaurant!" I whispered back, with flushed cheeks of my own. Though I had to admit, the idea of crawling under the table with him sparked a surprising thrill I'd never before considered. My lusty thoughts were quickly saved by a tray of hors-d'oeuvres the waiter brought to our table with impeccable timing. A beautiful golden crusted spinach pie served with tzatziki sauce and various types of hummus. Each were drizzled with fragrant, olive oil and topped with multi-colored olives that were finely chopped. The tray was accompanied by a basket filled with warm triangular cuts of freshly baked pita bread for dipping. The aroma was absolutely divine. I couldn't wait to take my taste buds on this tour as my mouth began to water without shame.

"Enjoy." The waiter said.

"Thank you, this looks great!" Jasper said to the waiter before he exited our booth.

By this time, the warm cherry currents of the wine had stained my lips and pitched a feverish tone to the rising current between Jasper and me. I was quickly led to anticipate more than just the feast before us. Jasper forked his way into the spinach pie offering it to my mouth for the first taste. I quickly obliged, opening up to catch the pastry before it fell off onto the table.

"Mmm... It's soo delicious!" I said in a half moan, dramatically defining the amusement of my taste buds.

"I knew you'd like it," Jasper smiled as he delivered a bite to his own mouth. "It's the best in the city," He added with his mouth full. We nearly finished the hummus and pita when the waiter came around with a second tray on his shoulder. This time he brought a tray stand with him to hold the heavy plates. There were three large plates filled with dishes I'd never seen before.

"Baby Lamb Chops marinated and seared in a fruity blend of garlic, olive oil, lemon juice, and topped with fresh oregano, served on a bed of Lemon Rice, Dolmas and Baked Moussaka. Try the mint jelly with the chops and please let us know if you'll be needing anything else to enhance your meal. Kali Oreksi!" Said the waiter as he presented our platters and extra plates.

"This looks perfect! Thank you," Jasper replied.

I had to admit, I was a bit overwhelmed being unfamiliar with the foods in front of me, but it all looked delicious! I'd never had lamb before, and was curious to know if I would enjoy it.

Everything tasted amazing, despite the fact that I was foreign to the dishes. The way Jasper described each morsel as he spooned them into my mouth for my first taste had me undoubtedly captivated by my tour guide. It was plain as day by anyone who may have been observing, that the heat was turned all the way up at our table. One could literally cut a knife through the sexual tension between us.

Towards the end of our meal, Jasper excused himself briefly to use the restroom. When the waiter passed by, I asked him to box up the rest of the food so we could bring home the leftovers. When Jasper returned, the waiter brought our boxes and asked if we wanted coffee. When he returned with our tray, he had a slew of staff trailing behind him with a giant slice of chocolate cake. They were all singing Happy Birthday so loud, the entire restaurant looked over and clapped when they were finished. I, of course, turned beet red, as I wasn't expecting them to sing to me. Jasper and I had a few bites from the towering cake before we asked to box up the rest to take home as well.

Chapter 23

My eyes lit up when we stepped outside. Standing before us, on the cobblestone street, was a great big white horse with two brown patches on his rear side. He was magnificent in size and was pulling a brown covered carriage behind him. Gauging my reaction, Jasper didn't miss a beat before asking the driver if we could climb aboard for a tour ride of Boston.

"I've never ridden in a horse and carriage before," I said excitedly to Jasper as he took my hand to boost me up inside the carriage.

"Me either, but I see them all the time up and down Main Street." Jasper said as he settled in beside me with all the bags of our leftovers from dinner.

The moon had fallen to a low hang in the sky. And though the lights of the city were bright, you could still see the twinkling of a few stars, as the carriage made its way over a small bridge. I was blissfully engaged in the sounds of the hoof steps when I dared myself to sink into the crook of Jasper's arms. He quickly reciprocated my motion with an outstretch of his magic fingers across my forearm to softly caress my skin. I took a second to relish in my contentment. *Is this for real? Could I be dreaming?* I wondered for a moment as I inhaled the crisp, cool night air. Jasper pointed over to the lighthouse we could see, off in the distance, across the water. "I used to climb up to the top when I was a teenager and watch the waves of the sea. Whenever life didn't seem to make sense, I would go there to feel closer to my dad."

"Aww, that's sweet. Did it ever help you feel better?" I asked.

"Usually it did. Between the distraction of the climb and the view from up top, I suppose." Jasper replied, pensively. "Who knows if he was ever really listening. I was just a kid."

"I'm sure he was. I honestly believe we are connected to the people we love in spirit. Bonds that strong can never be broken. I feel my grandmother's spirit with me all the time," I said.

"That's an interesting perspective. I never thought about it like that before." Jasper said as he tugged me in a little closer and took a deep breath of the salty air. "There's a lake house property for sale on the other side I have been thinking about buying. It's only a five minute walk to the lighthouse. I really like it, but it does need a lot of work. Maybe I'll take you to see it sometime."

"I'd like that," I said as my phone rang out of nowhere, breaking the cocoon of bliss I was in. I loved that Jasper was opening up to me again and hoped I was doing enough of the same in return. I quickly pulled my phone out of my purse to find Ben's name flashing across the screen. *What could he possibly want at this hour of the night?* It should be noted that it was only 9 PM. Still a strange time to be hearing from

Ben. I was already in enough heat with him and figured it best to answer his call if I wanted any chance at keeping my job at the coffee shop.

"Ben! Hi! How are you?" I asked in an easy to detect, schmoozy tone.

"Save it, girly! I need you to open for me tomorrow. Brooke told me you were back in town. Ashley has the stomach flu and you owe me big time!" He said, clearly more concerned with me saving his ass than how I've been and what I'd been through. It was callous, sure, but also nothing I wouldn't expect of him. To be honest, I was more thrilled for the chance at making it up to him and getting my ass out of the hot seat. This was my opportunity to keep the job I'd quickly grown fond of.

"Okay." I replied. "I'll be there." I heard a sigh of relief come through Ben's end of the line.

"I knew you were a smart girl!" He said. "OK, that's all, thanks! Bye!" and as quick as the call came in, the line went dead.

"Who's Ben?" Jasper was quick to ask with a raise of his eyebrow.

"Ben is my manager at my job at the coffee shop. He needs me to work tomorrow." Jasper's expression clearly defined his disappointment.

"Oh…. Does this mean you're not staying over tonight? I was really hoping to have a reason to play hooky tomorrow." I had to admit, the tag-team wink and smirk were very persuasive, especially when that lonely dimple came to surface on his left cheek.

"I really should stay home tonight. It is my first night back in town and Jamie and I have some catching up to do. Believe it or not, I'm actually excited to get back in the swing of things," I replied to Jasper as we drew near to our stop. "I honestly can't remember a time when I enjoyed myself as much as I have, though. Thank you so much for making me feel so special." Truthfully, I couldn't wait to put this entire night down on paper in my Never Forget Journal.

Jasper was the first one out of the carriage. He offered his hand to help me down onto the cobblestone street and handed the driver a folded wad of bills. "Impeccable timing, buddy! Thanks so much for the ride!"

"My pleasure! Anytime, anytime!" The driver replied back. His eyes twinkled in the moonlight as he was clearly happy with his compensation.

The night time air had dipped into the lower 60s and I began to shiver when the wind picked up. Jasper quickly pulled his jacket off and covered my shoulders with it.

"Well, we're here. Let's get you inside before you catch a cold." He said as he guided me by hand to the entrance of our apartment building.

~

With Jasper's hand at the small of my back, I could feel the tension rising between us when we stepped onto the elevator. The electrifying pulse of his touch made me want to reconsider my decision to go home for the night. My nerves had my eyes settling on the numbers of the floors displayed across the top of the elevator as we passed each one at what seemed like snail speed. Jasper abruptly stole my attention away from the screen when he carefully set the bags with our leftovers on the floor of the elevator and hit the stop button. He pinned me up against the elevator wall in one swift move.

"Are you sure I can't sway your decision?" He asked in a hot whisper to my ear... "Just for a little while?" He pressed his body into me so I could feel his erection at my belly button. I was already flustered by the intensity of the energy flowing between us inside the confines of the elevator. I swear, we could make this thing move all on our own.

"You're killing me." I squeaked out as he stifled my words with his lips. His skillful hands making their way up my thigh stopping to settle on my ass as he gave it a light squeeze. He deepened the kiss to solidify his request. *How could I ever resist?* In a tit for tat, I kissed him back, quickly exchanging the fever I had been assaulted with. It took everything in me to break away from his embrace. I pressed my fists against his chest, silently pleading for him to release me. He gazed deep into my eyes and stepped back as I hazily inhaled a short breath to regather my senses.

"As hard as it is for me to say this..." I let out a deep sigh. "I really want to catch Jamie before she goes to bed. If I go upstairs with you, I already know I won't make it back home," I admitted.

"If that's what you really want, Angel... Say no more." He said as he released the stop button on the elevator. *What I wanted was to ride this train as far as it would go, but I had to be responsible. This was my only chance to prove to Ben that I could be relied upon.* Besides, I knew I was far too weak to resist Jasper and his adept moves. Not that this was bad at all. I secretly loved how effective he was at keeping me enamored. I just couldn't risk not making it to work on time the next morning.

"Please?" I asked, with my biggest puppy dog eyes. "I hope you're not mad."

"Not at all, Angel. You're adorable when you beg." He said with a small smile and his deep blue eyes aglow. "I can wait... But I will have you again soon, make no mistake about that."

The elevator dinged, alerting us to Jamie's floor as the doors began to open. Jasper walked me over to the front door of Jamie's apartment and gave me a sweet soft peck on my lips. "Sweet Dreams, Baby. Text me when you get a break." He said before turning on his heels.

"Good night, Jasper... And thanks again for everything!" I called out.

"The pleasure was all mine, Angel." I heard him reply in response before disappearing behind the elevator doors.

Chapter 24

I entered the apartment to find Jamie half asleep on the couch surrounded by random popcorn kernels that had fallen from the bowl she had been eating them out of. The remote control lay across her lap over the blanket she was snuggled up in. As I edged my way closer to the sofa, I noticed she had left a few sips of wine inside her glass that sat on the side table.

Clips from The Notebook rang out through the sound bar as Jamie moaned her greeting to me through her nostrils. It was evident she was tipsy from the wine when she wiggled herself up into a seated position on the couch. "Hey you... How did it go?" She asked as she stretched out a yawn.

I was still heady from the rush of Jasper's kiss he had left me with in his departure. The delicious scent of his cologne still lingered within the fibers of his jacket, of which I was still wearing. My entire being was enraptured with his presence. "Oh my gosh... It was so good. Better than I could ever have imagined." Jamie's eyebrows raised in amusement. It was obvious she wanted me to spare no details when she asked me to continue without words.

"So... He took me to this amazing Greek restaurant. The food and service was fantastic! The entire wait staff sang to me when they brought me a giant piece of chocolate cake for my birthday, which by the way, was honestly to die for!" I said with a deep sigh of contentment as the remnants of the evening still lingered on in my mind. "And as if that weren't enough, we actually rode home in a horse and carriage. It was all so incredibly romantic!" I hummed out, clearly pleasured by the details of my night.

"Wow... Sounds like you two had quite the night! Did you guys talk at all about what happened between you and Tommy?" She asked, quickly sobering me from my current state of ecstasy. The tinge of butterflies awakened in my tummy as I recalled the only time the subject was brushed upon. I wouldn't go that far into details, but I could give her enough to fill the space in her mind where she was curious.

"Let's just say it was squashed the moment he clearly defined what our relationship actually meant to him." I said with a gleam in my eyes that said way more than my words could ever.

"Oh... " I watched the line between her eyebrows furrow with curiosity. "Well.. Don't stop now! What did he say?" She asked.

"Basically that I was his and he was mine. And! He would soon prove to me just how much he meant it so there won't be any more confusion" I replied.

"Interesting... What about the girl from the club? Did that come up at all?" She asked. Clearly the wine had her in a state of speculation.

I could see now that she needed closure on that particular situation in order to fully believe everything that he was telling me. Truthfully, I did too, but something inside me was telling me that I could trust Jasper. I don't know why, but my instincts had always felt this way about him from the moment I first laid eyes on him, that day at the park. I could hardly blame her for wanting to protect me though, especially after everything I had gone through with AJ. I would feel the same way about her if the situation had been reversed.

"I didn't ask him. Honestly, I'm really excited that we are in a good place right now. I really don't want to come off the wrong way by being so intrusive this early on in our relationship. I think I'm just going to give it more time to see if anything else comes to surface. But I will be keeping my eyes open for any red flags." I reassured her.

"Well, I am happy for you. I just want to make sure you don't get hurt, that's all." She said as she reached over and finished what was left in her glass of wine.

"I know." I said, looking around for something to change the subject. "So where is Dillon? Did he leave?"

"Yes… He left here about an hour ago to head back home," She replied.

"And how did everything go with you two?" I asked. I was genuinely curious and wanted to catch up on her relationship, but also needed something to distract the speculative state she seemed to be in about mine.

"We had a great time. Round two was even better than the first!" She said with a devilish grin that left absolutely nothing to my imagination.

"Obviously, I was sad to see him leave, but he did say he would try to rearrange some appointments so he could come and see me again this weekend," She replied with a smile. It was hard not to notice the sparkle in her eyes. I wasn't sure if it was the wine or the fact that she seemed genuinely happy but she looked positively radiant in the glowing aura that surrounded her. Either way, it was plain to see her contentment in the relationship she was building with Dillon.

"That's great! Ooh, you know what might be really fun?" I asked. "Maybe we can arrange a double date this weekend." Clearly I was just as excited about my own relationship and the fact that we both had boyfriends at the same time for once, which never seemed to happen in the past. We were both so used to playing the third wheel in each other's previous relationships.

"That sounds like a great idea. I'll talk to Dillon about it tomorrow." She agreed.

"Sweet!" I said. "Well, I think I'd better turn in for the night. Ben, my manager at the coffee shop, called me earlier. He needs me to open in the morning. Apparently Ashley has a stomach virus and won't be able to come in tomorrow."

"Well, I'm glad you told me. Now I know to make sure you're up in the morning. It's probably time I turn in as well. I need to be up early too." She said as she propped herself up off the couch. "I'll clean this up tomorrow." She giggled as she caught sight of all the popcorn kernels that fell.

~

I spent the next 45 minutes scribbling every little detail of my night with Jasper into my Never Forget journal. By the time I was finished it was 11:30. Tomorrow was a big day for me, as I would finally get back into the swing of work. I needed to bring my A-game if I wanted to find myself back within the good graces of both of my jobs. I really wanted to let them know that I could be relied upon as an employee. It pained me to no end that I had to begin on such a rocky start.

I turned off the light from the lamp on the bedside table and put my journal inside the drawer. I sent Jasper a quick text before hopping into bed to thank him for such a beautiful homecoming. I resonated deep within the memory of my night that had been freshly painted in my mind from writing it all down and fell fast asleep.

Chapter 25

Jasper

After taking Lucas out for his nightly walk, I settled upstairs in the loft to relax for a bit before going to bed. I found Carla's text message when I plugged my phone into the charger for the night. I sent her a quick reply to let her know the pleasure was all mine, but she never texted me back. It was almost midnight, so I figured she had already gone to bed.

God, it felt so good to be inside her... If only she knew how much it tore me to shreds when she told me she kissed another guy after I left her in Virginia. If only I had given her my full attention, the attention she truly deserves. Maybe then, she wouldn't have been driven straight into the arms of another man. And all because of my dumb ass mistakes.

I may have done a fair enough job in masking the agony I felt with everything I'm up against tonight, but that still didn't change the fact that I felt like a real prick for keeping it all to myself. Keeping this secret from her was killing me. Whether I had a choice in the matter or not did absolutely nothing for my guilt ridden conscience. Before I got that call, my relationship with Carla was moving in such a positive direction. She was finally free from the situation with AJ. The last thing we needed right now was more drama.

When I first met Lena, I knew that she was trouble. I could see that in her swaying eyes. The way she looked at me any chance she had, whenever Sam wasn't looking. Sam seemed so enamored by her, though. I just couldn't bring myself to crush his dreams with my silly suspicions. *What if I was wrong?* Coming between them and his happiness was the furthest from my mind, despite my own terrible luck in the love department. I was still happy to see my friend excited to have found someone he could truly love. The way she had her eye on me made it very clear, however, the adoration traveled down a one-way street between them.

After all that Carla went through this past week, I just knew I had to shield her from this. She'd clearly been through enough. Besides, I was far from ready to let her in on my tumultuous sexual behavior prior to meeting her. *Christ, I don't know if I would ever be ready for that!* She had this purity about her. It was honestly what drew me to her the most. *My Angel.* The moment I laid eyes on her, I just knew she had been sent here to save me. *The question was, was I even worth saving?*

No amount of video games would settle my tormented mind. *Fuck!* I could barely even think straight. I wanted to be near her so badly! Not only was I keeping this secret from her, a secret that could possibly destroy us and everything we were building, betraying her trust by pretending everything was alright was damn near eating me alive.

One thing was certain… I didn't have all that long to figure things out. Even though she may not have picked up on it tonight, I knew she was everything she claimed to be; that she had a gift to see things beyond the surface. I could feel it in our intimacy. How she lights up whenever I set my eyes on her, it was all a reflection of how she made me feel inside.

I knew I couldn't be so lucky to have found her as I had initially thought. No, this… this was my own fucking karma. *I knew I didn't deserve her.* This was for all the hearts I had broken along the way. To know that everything I had ever needed was finally here, right in front of me and that one false move had the potential to take it all away. I had to be cautious in my steps. For now, until I could figure out exactly what I was facing, I would have to wear this stupid mask and hope I could continue on with my charade of making things appear as if everything was perfectly fine. *I'm going to hell for this, I'm sure!* I thought as I huffed out a deep breath of frustration and threw the XBOX controller down on the carpet in front of me. I headed for the cabinet in search of my bottle of scotch, took a swig and went to bed, not even caring that Lucas followed me. Hell, at least it was a warm body and I could just close my eyes and pretend it was her to help me fall asleep.

Chapter 26

⸺ ∽❀∾ ⸺

Carla

An eerie feeling crept over me when I stepped outside into the cool morning air. The darkened night sky had fallen into a purplish-orange hue as the sun just barely began to peek out from the horizon. There was a silent, stillness to the air that left traces of impending danger. Even the birds were stagnantly quiet. It was as if they, too, were conspiring along with me in my sixth sense that something might be terribly wrong.

My instincts quickly reminded me of my training session to be fully aware of my surroundings. And from all that I could see, there was nothing I could put my finger on that could land the role of a suspect. A few cars had passed me by, though that was nothing new for the early morning hours I was used to when I would typically walk to work. The only people I could see were a man walking his poodle and a mama walking her baby in a stroller across the street. I still couldn't shake the distinct feeling that I was being followed.

I picked up my pace and gripped my finger on the trigger of the pepper spray that was hooked into the belt loop of the waistline of my jeans. I was only a few minutes away. Surely, I could make it to safety once I got to the coffee shop, where I would soon be met with whoever it was that would work the morning shift with me.

The bookstore was closed as usual, as they didn't open up until 9 AM. I unlocked the side entrance to the coffee shop and went inside. I didn't know who else was scheduled to work with me as Mondays were typically my day off at the coffee shop. Whoever it was picked the wrong day to be late, that's for sure! I thought to myself as I locked the door behind me and went about my typical opening procedures.

My heart nearly fell out of my chest when Aaron finally showed up, banging on the side door for me to let him in. I quickly ran to unlock the door.

"You're late!" I said in a tone that let him know just how annoyed I was. "Most of the side work is done, you can finish the rest while I run to the restroom," I said. I handed him the container of milk I had been filling the canisters with.

"Where's Ashley?" He called out as I made a beeline to the bathroom.

"She's sick!" I replied as I walked through the door and closed it behind me. I took a second to catch my breath and turned on the faucet to splash some cold water on my face. I needed to get a grip on myself before the crowds started pouring in for their morning coffee. Perhaps I was letting my imagination get the best of me. I took a quick glance at my reflection in the mirror. *You're fine, Carla. Let it go!* I said to myself as I pulled my phone out of my back pocket. I found Jasper's reply to my text message from last night. I smiled instantly as a sense of calmness finally helped me relax my mind. I typed a quick message in response and hit send before stuffing my phone back into the back pocket of my jeans.

Me:

Good morning ;) Just got to work, I'll text you later! Hope you have a great day! Xo

There was already a line forming at the door when I unlocked it to let our patrons in. Thankfully Aaron was a quick start, despite his being late. We had never worked together previously, but I had seen him a time or 2 before. Once when he came in to get his check, the other was to relieve me of my shift. We seemed to work well enough together, though he was not nearly as friendly as Brooke had always been with me.

When Ben showed up at 9:30 AM, I was the first to take my break. I stopped dead in my tracks when I started to open the door to go outside. There she was, sitting on the bench across the street with her eyes set straight in my direction. The blonde bimbo from the club and without an actual name for her, that's all I could use to describe who she was. At least for the time being until I could find out more about her. Only that wouldn't happen unless Jasper decided to spill the beans about who she was.

Was she watching me? Had it been her who was following me this morning? Why on earth would she be following me, anyway? Perhaps it was all just some crazy coincidence led by my creative imagination. Although I may have been dying to know if she was following me and why, the last thing I would do was give her what she wanted if she was. I quickly turned on my heels and took my breakfast over to one of the chairs inside the bookstore in place of my original plans to walk over to the park.

I tried to let it go and just read, but my mind couldn't seem to focus on anything else but *her!* The words in the pages all seemed to fall upon deaf ears as I hadn't truly processed a single 1, despite my greatest efforts of distracting my mind and where it was going. *Stop overthinking, Carla!* I told myself as I shoved the last bite of my sandwich into my mouth and stood up to get back to work.

The morning rush had slowed down quite a bit and I could still see her sitting on the bench through the window. *What was she just gonna do, just sit there all day?!* I wondered. I really wished that Brooke was here with me. At least I could talk to her about everything I was going through. I laughed as I imagined the stance she might take. *Would she think I was being completely irrational or play detective right along with me?* I wondered. At the very least, I could have talked her into going to lunch with me afterwards so I wouldn't have to walk home, alone.

By the time my shift ended, I was relieved when I noticed that "Blonde Bimbo" had finally left and took the sense that I was being followed right along with her. *Thank God!* I walked home, exhausted from everywhere my mind had traveled. My feet were tired and sore and I just wanted to lay down for a bit before I had to leave for work again at Silver Linings.

Chapter 27

Maggie welcomed me with open arms when I arrived at Silver Linings. She didn't press me much, but I could tell she was happy to see my return. Her sweet, caring voice set a tone for the calmness that would follow my first day back at the office. I should've known there might be a welcome cake... but I was surprised anyway when I found it sitting on the kitchen counter of our break room. "Welcome Back Carla" was written across the top. There was also a note card placed in front warning everyone to back off until I got the first slice.

A bouquet of vibrant yellow sunflowers shouted out for my attention where they stood inside a large vase, behind the cake. The navy blue ribbon tied around the vase held an envelope with my name written on it as well. I carefully removed the envelope to read the card.

CARLA,

THESE ARE FOR YOU TO TAKE HOME...
    WE MISSED YOU!

WELCOME BACK, ANGEL

The back of the card was signed by everyone in the office, but I could tell that it was Jasper who had written it, because he called me "Angel". My heart fluttered just thinking about him. This was such a sweet gesture and made me feel so much better about having to take the time away that I needed.

He knew that I was worried about how my departure would have been received by Maggie and all of my new coworkers. I figured it might feel awkward to see him at the office after the secret of our relationship was revealed but my heart still longed to be near him, regardless of any tension I might face.

I hadn't seen him at all since my arrival at the office, which was normal, because my shift didn't begin until after he typically left. Just seeing him call me *"Angel"* on the card brought me butterflies and a deep longing, as the memory of our last encounter flashed through my mind. I was reminded of the urgency I felt in his presence when he first grabbed a hold of me in his apartment and then again in the elevator before I went home. It was all so incredibly sexy and still had me reeling for his touch, even now, right here in the freaking break room.

The magnetic pull this man had on me was a force to be reckoned with for sure. I let myself lather up in appreciation for what it truly was. No man, in the 24 years I had stood on this earth, had ever had this type of effect on me before. The memory of last night, alone, continued to walk with me in the dreamy state he always seemed to put me in. I needed to settle my ass down before I got caught, so I did the only thing I could think of to distract my wayward thoughts and cut myself a hefty slice of cake.

Mmm, Delicious! I thought to myself as I spooned a bite into my mouth. It almost felt sinful, sitting there alone in the break room, indulging in the vanilla cake topped with homemade buttercream icing and fresh blueberries laced between each layer. *You deserve it, Angel.* I could almost hear Jasper's voice whispering in my ear as I savored my last bite. I quickly cleaned up my mess of crumbs on the table before heading back to my work station.

The phone lines were oddly quiet for the most part of the day. I couldn't help myself from lapping up every inch of the daydream I was in and the charmingly seductive hold that Jasper still had on me from our previous night, together. It baffled me just how incredibly connected to him I was feeling, even in the absence of his physical presence. It was as if he had been tattooed on my mind, a permanent imprint I was more than happy to have acquired. I still couldn't help but wonder if our meeting had been touched by the divine. As if we were created specifically for one another, somehow.

Even though our relationship was still very new, I thought this feeling would have subsided a bit, at least by now, anyway. Especially after spending the significant amount of time together that we did while we were in Virginia. It was spellbinding, actually... The infusion of electricity that pulsed through me at every thought that he was in felt so incredibly surreal, just as it had that first day I laid eyes on him. It was almost as if my soul was completely possessed by his admiration of me.

And I was just as captivated by him as he was of me. Though I wondered if I had expressed that enough. I had always been shy and reserved about my feelings and emotions, it was just in my nature to be this way. My feelings ran dangerously, deep, despite my lack of verbal communication. So deep, I felt the need to protect them with everything I had. I was soon led to wonder if I was sharing enough with my unspoken words to satisfy his need to hear them. Surely, I could conjure up a way to show him that I was thrilled to know that "I was his" as he had so graciously reminded me of when we last made love.

My feelings were always better communicated on paper than spoken; I could never seem to put the words together by mouth without sounding like an incoherent mess. Regardless of my flaws that I was highly conscious of, I knew it was time to make a statement of my own to let him know that I was out there on the rope with him in terms of vulnerability. He wasn't acting as if he felt insecure about us on our date, but I could sense it in the urgency of his touch. It was as if he craved my affection to soothe his need of knowing I was truly his.

With the extra time I had, I began a search on the internet in hopes to find something I could possibly purchase for him. By now, he had already given me so many gifts and I hadn't done anything in return, aside from baking him a cake. Perhaps I was still on guard from the aftermath of my relationship with AJ.

Something clicked inside me, however, the night that Tommy kissed me. He made me realize that Jasper was truly what my heart was longing for. I knew from that moment on that he was it for me. There was no doubt about it, Jasper was my person.

I had no clue where to begin when it came to buying him a gift, though. *I mean, what do you buy for someone who already has everything they need?*

It would have to be a gift of sentiment.

After scrolling through a generic search of gift ideas for men, nothing seemed to hit my mark. I finally settled on a hot dog toy for Lucas. It was cute and funny and I was sure he would catch my reference. My true message to him would be in the card that I would pour my heart into, in my true hallmark fashion. If I truly wanted to share my most intimate feelings with Jasper, I knew I would have to seek them out through my writing.

Chapter 28

As the sun began to set in the crystal blue sky, my seemingly long shift had finally come to an end. I gathered my bag and the bouquet of sunflowers that had been gifted to me and headed out to my car. I needed to find something to secure the vase from falling down on my drive back home. I stopped dead in my tracks when I found the words "Go home" written in the dust that had settled on the back of my trunk.

Instantly, I felt the tiny little hairs on the back of my neck stand up as panic quickly spread through me like a wildfire. I just stood there stunned, momentarily wondering if this could have been done by someone here on the Silver Linings property. *No way!* This place is way too protected and everyone here seemed genuinely nice to me. Besides that, all of the residents here had their own issues to deal with and were recovering from their own lives to have any motive to scare me like this. I was pretty sure I would know if it were someone in the office. I was way too perceptive to not be aware if someone might have had it out for me.

I hadn't noticed it before I left for work, where it was parked inside the garage of the apartment building, but I also wasn't able to catch the angle I could see it from now. My heart began to race as my mind began to cross examine everyone I had come in contact with since I had come back to Boston. There weren't very many, only Jamie, Dillon, Jasper and my coworkers for the most part. None of them gave me any reason to believe it could have been any one of them.

The eerie feeling I had from this morning struck me all over again. Perhaps I really was being followed as I had initially thought. After checking the rest of my car thoroughly, thankfully finding nothing else of concern, I placed the vase in the front seat of my car and secured it with a sweater I found inside my trunk. I turned on the ignition and quickly stepped away from my car to ensure it wasn't going to blow up or anything. *Get a grip! It's probably just some kids playing around or something.* I laughed nervously at myself as I got in my car to head home for the night.

When I got home, Jamie was in the kitchen scouring the contents of the fridge to try and find something to cook us for dinner.

"We need to go shopping." She said, before slamming the refrigerator door shut in frustration. "Wanna take a walk up to the market with me?" She asked, her eyes widened when she saw me set the sunflowers onto the dining room table.

"Yeah, okay." I said, still stirred from what had occurred before I left work.

"You okay, hon? What's wrong?" She asked, quickly detecting the shakiness in my voice.

"I'm sure it's nothing. It's fine. I'm fine." I said, trying to make light of the heavy situation I was in. I wasn't sure who I was trying to convince more, Jamie or myself.

"Just tell me, Carla. I'm no fool. I can tell when something is wrong." She implored as she eyed me for any further clues. I was definitely done for now! I may as well just come out with it.

Being a writer, I was never good at telling stories, but I gave it my best. "So, this morning, I had this strange feeling on my way to work like someone was following me. Well, that turned out to be nothing, so I let it go." I glanced over at Jamie who was patiently waiting for me to finish. "So, when I left work tonight at Silver Linings, I found the words "Go Home" written on the back of my trunk. And, I don't know, I'm sure it's nothing. Probably just some kids playing around, I'm sure."

"Wow, well, that's definitely not nothing. You have every reason to be shaken up. I know I would be if it had happened to me," She said, validating everything I was feeling, like any good best friend would do. "Do you have any idea when it was written? Is it possible that it could've happened while you were up in Virginia?" She had a valid point. I tried to retrace my steps when I left for Boston.

"No, I remember loading my bags inside the trunk before I said Goodbye to Mama and Abby. I definitely would have noticed it then, if it was. No, it had to be here. But I haven't the slightest clue as to who would want to do that."

"I see. Well, I'm sure we'll get to the bottom of it somehow," She said as she scooped up her purse from the dining room table and tossed it over her shoulder. "Maybe something else might jog your memory."

"I keep telling myself it's probably just a prank from some punk teenagers," I said as I followed her out the door.

"I sure hope you're right." Jamie said.

~

Jamie and I stopped by to see Freddie, the security guard, on our way out. He told us that in order to pull the security camera footage, he would have to talk to his supervisor.

"I'm afraid that without a specific time frame it could take some time to comb through, Miss." I watched his eyebrows arch into what appeared to be genuine concern. "I'll see what I can find out for you." He added in a scrambled attempt to reassure us as best he could.

Dusk had settled into the night. The dusty gray clouds set high in the sky offered a blanket to the moon in its wake. The air was clear and cool and the city appeared to have a docile demeanor when Jamie and I headed out into the street. It was a beautiful backdrop for our walk up to the corner store.

"Maybe we should see about getting you something to protect yourself. Something a little stronger than pepper spray. I hate that you walk to work so early in the morning by yourself." Jamie turned to me and said.

"I'll be fine, Jamie. God forbid if anything were to ever happen, I could always scream. Believe it or not, there's usually people out and about in the early morning hours. Plus, I really enjoy my morning walk, it helps me wake up." I paused briefly to consider what she was actually saying. "I mean, it's not like I would carry a gun or anything like that!" I laughed.

"Why not?" She asked.

"You know I hate guns. No one should ever have that much power over anybody."

"Fair point, but I would still feel better knowing that you had something to protect yourself, just in case of anything. It does seem silly to drive and have to look for parking when your job is so close... I just worry about you, is all. What about a knife?" She said as we approached the market.

"I suppose a knife would be something I might consider. Not that I like those either." I laughed, but it seemed a fair compromise. Honestly, I had my doubts that I could ever bring myself to actually use it, but there was also no way it might go off unintentionally either. A knife did sound like a safer alternative to me. Especially if it made her feel better.

"Have you talked to Jasper about what happened yet?" She asked.

"No. I haven't. Actually, I haven't heard from him all day. I thought for sure I might catch him at work, but he had already left for the day. He did leave me those sunflowers though. He even had everyone in the office sign a card to welcome me back. You should've seen it, they actually baked me another cake! It was so good too, Blueberry Shortcake!" I said, deeply delighted by my recollection of that stolen moment in the break room. I could almost feel the glow in my own smile. I found it fascinating that my entire energy had shifted just by thinking about him.

"Aww, that was so sweet of him!" She agreed, clearly impressed by his gesture and the reaction I had towards it.

"You guys are so stinkin' adorable!" Her words made me blush.

After gathering a few groceries we could easily take home with us on our walk, we decided on making some sub sandwiches for dinner to make it an easy night. I stopped by the stationary aisle to pick out the card I wanted to give to Jasper and Lucas's toy was already on its way to be delivered by tomorrow.

Chapter 29

O n our walk back to Jamie's apartment, my body felt like
it was floating on air. It was like my spirit was dancing
underneath the pale, blue light of the moon that had since
crept out from underneath the blanket of clouds that were invading
the sky on our way up to the market. I didn't know what got into me,
but by the time we turned the corner to where our apartment building
stood, I soon had my answer.

"Speak of the devil." Jamie said as she turned her head in my direction
so that only I could hear.

In a matter of seconds, I had a very large gray dog at my feet with a
leash attached to no one. And one gorgeous blue-eyed Jasper trailing
in the flight of its digression. *God he was hot!* My lust-filled eyes felt
like they were sinning just staring at him.

"Evening, ladies!" Jasper said, as he gracefully caught his breath and
took hold of Lucas's leash. I had been quick to step on it to keep him
from running out into the street.

"Apparently someone really misses you." Jasper chuckled. By now, I was crouched down, deeply engaged with smooches from the giant pup. Jamie quickly gathered the bag of apples that had fallen out of the grocery bag I had been holding onto when I was toppled by the beast, also known as Lucas.

"Hi Angel." Jasper said, meeting me at my level to peck me on the top of my head as Lucas had already taken sole proprietorship of my face. When I finally got Lucas to settle down, I could see Jamie's eyes twinkle as she had taken in quite the scene of affection towards me.

"You wanna come for a walk with us?" Jasper asked me.

"Oh... Well, you know I would love to," I started to reply as I shuffled my feet. I quickly exchanged glances with Jamie, "but we just got home with our dinner and groceries."

"Oh, right." Jasper said, as he gained some insight of his surroundings.

"Don't worry about the groceries! I got this." Jamie quickly chimed in as she pried the bag I was able to keep a hold of from out of my hand. "Go ahead... I'll have your sandwich ready for you when you come back." She reiterated.

"Are you sure?" I asked.

"Yes I'm sure. Sure as the sun will come out tomorrow, you can bet your bottom dollar on that!" She said, smiling. I adored her reference to my all time favorite movie, Annie!

"Oh my God, I freakin' love you Jamie!" I beamed as I watched her head for the door of the lobby.

"Love you too, sis!" She called back. "Go, have fun you two!"

"We just came down a minute ago. I was gonna take him to the park, if you want to come along." He said.

"Yeah... That sounds nice. How was your day today?" I asked, curiously, as we trailed Lucas across the cobblestone street. Jasper wrapped Lucas's leash tightly around his fist another time to secure his grip.

"Not bad... How about you? Did you get the flowers I left you?" He asked.

"Yes! I love them! Thank you so much! You have no idea how much better I feel knowing that my return to work would be so welcoming. It honestly made my day!" I said, smiling. "And that cake was absolutely to die for!"

"What cake? I didn't get any cake!" Jasper frowned dramatically, then quickly withdrew when he flashed me that sexy grin that showcased his dimple. The one that always made me melt whenever I saw it.

"Of course, anything for my Angel." He draped his arm around my shoulder when we approached the entrance of the park. The street lights were all lit up and this was the first time I had seen the park in a nighttime setting. It was quiet, though. Some runners zipped past us and there was an older lady sitting on the bench, feeding the ducks. The moon light shimmered its reflection in the water of the pond, illuminating the magic I felt inside me as it continued its flow, back and forth between us.

"You know, that's too bad, because you totally missed out!" I said in direct combat with his charm.

"They were trying to decide between strawberries and blueberries before I left. My vote went to the blueberries." He smiled. "I had a meeting and couldn't stay long enough for them to finish. I told Maggie to save me a piece for tomorrow. Hopefully it's still there in the fridge when I get there in the morning." He said with a cross of his fingers.

"I sure hope so, for your sake!" I laughed. "No, but honestly, that was really very sweet of you to make my first day back so special. I really appreciate it. And I'll keep the winner of the berries a surprise for you." I said with a wink.

"You know you are so damn sexy when you flirt!" He said. I blushed at his remark.

"Who? Me?" I laughed. "I do not have a single flirt bone in my body." I recounted.

"Says you! The one who's got me all hot and bothered out here in a public place. I swear, if I didn't have Lucas with me, I would pull you behind those bushes over there and prove it to you." He growled. I gulped. The heat of his words hit me deep within my core, arousing the butterflies to a rampant frenzy. I could barely catch my breath to come back.

"Our champion, chaperon, at his best! Thanks Lucas!" I said, patting Lucas on the top of his head. My affection was quickly returned with a giant lick to my hand and a nudge of his nose for me to pet him.

We walked around the park for a little while until Lucas finished his business, then headed back to the apartment. For a moment, I had the strangest feeling that we were being watched, but I couldn't see anyone around that looked suspicious. I hadn't decided if I should tell Jasper about the incident with my car. I knew he had his own stuff he was dealing with, which was all still a nagging mystery to me. But I promised myself I wouldn't dig too deep. So far, there weren't any other clues that had risen to the surface, but also nothing to strike me to be concerned, other than an exchange of the urgency I felt when he made love to me when I got back to Boston. Whatever it was could have been anything at this point and may have already been settled by now. I figured I may as well just let it go.

We cornered our way to the apartment building and walked in through the lobby. Freddie, the security guard, was still there. *Shit!* I ducked behind Jasper as we made our way past the front desk so he wouldn't call me over to discuss what Jamie and I had talked to him about earlier that evening. I really didn't want to cause Jasper any concern.

"Evening, Sir." Freddie said to Jasper as I casually ran to press the elevator button.

"How's it going, Freddie?" Jasper asked with a nod to Freddie in acknowledgment.

"Another beautiful night. I can't complain." Freddie replied.

The ding of the elevator could not have come at a better time. Lucas quickly followed right behind me, dragging Jasper away from the front desk.

"Where are you off to in such a hurry?" Jasper asked with a chuckle. Apparently I was not so smooth in my attempt to avoid the situation from escalating. I needed to think fast to recover.

"Nowhere, I'm just really hungry." I said, laughing nervously.

"Are you okay?" He asked me in a curious tone.

"I'm good," I said. "I just get really nervous whenever we share an elevator together, now. Thanks to you." *There! That should do it!* I smiled, silently patting myself on the back for my deflective reply.

"Did you forget we have our chaperon present?" He recanted.

"How could I ever forget this cutie pie?" I replied, as I lowered to face level with Lucas. He quickly plastered my face with kisses. And the elevator alerted us to the floor of Jamie's apartment. Jasper held his hand out to keep the elevator doors from closing in on me.

"Have you had dinner yet?" I asked. "We're just making sandwiches tonight but you're welcome to come down if you'd like. I'm sure Jamie won't mind, we have plenty enough if you're hungry."

"I need to make a few phone calls, otherwise, I would." He replied. "Maybe we can have dinner tomorrow night? My place?" He asked.

"Oh… Ok, then. Yeah, sure. That sounds nice." I said nervously.

"It's a date. Good night, Angel." He grabbed my arm, pulling me closer to tug my chin in his direction and kissed me. *Gosh! What is it about these elevator kisses?!* I nearly stumbled on my way to Jamie's front door.

I don't know what it was, but there was something about the way he said goodbye that left me wondering where his mind was at. That kiss though! I had been recharged with that same electric current. It coursed through me so hard, I could bet money on the fact that I might have trouble sleeping that night.

Chapter 30

J amie was settled on the couch with her sandwich when I walked through the door.

"Hey... How did *that* go?!" She eyed me curiously before taking a generous bite of her sandwich. "By the way, your dinner is on the kitchen counter." She said, with her mouthful.

"It went good, we walked Lucas over to the park." I replied. "I didn't tell him about the incident with my car. I don't want to worry him right now with all that he has going on." Jamie gave me an understanding nod as she continued to chew what was inside her mouth.

"I feel bad that we never got to celebrate your birthday, maybe we can do it this Friday, instead, what do you think?" Jamie asked, excitedly.

"Sure... but you really don't have to, you know. You've got so much going on already with work and school." I replied.

"I know that, silly girl. But it's not fair that you never got the celebration you deserve. He took enough from you already, don't let him have this too!" I couldn't argue with her.

"You're right, okay. But you don't have to go all out." I said, taking my plate with me to sit with her on the couch. "You didn't put cheese on it, did you?"

"Come on, you know me better than that, don't you?" Jamie asked.

"Well, I do love cheese, even though I shouldn't have it. I just don't want to wake up with a headache, especially since I have to work in the morning." I said as I unhinged the TV tray table to set my dinner on. I sat down next to Jamie and took a bite of my sandwich. Shaved, lean, rare roast beef with lettuce, tomato, mayo and sub dressing on a bakery fresh multigrain sub roll. Jamie made it perfectly, just the way I like it with all the veggies chopped! "Mmm... It's so good! Thank you, Jamie." I really was starving.

Jamie had Annie loaded in the DVD player for us to watch. Once I was settled, she pressed play on the remote control. We both sang along to all the songs and ate some not so terrible vanilla vegan cupcakes we were dying to try for dessert. When the movie was over, we both went to bed.

Just as I imagined, I did have trouble falling asleep. My head was spinning, trying to decipher the emotions I was feeling. I was so used to keeping my calm, cool, collective demeanor to face the world with. My feelings often shouted out their existence to me in an intense overtaking of my mind whenever I suppressed them for too long. *Why am I so afraid to express how I'm feeling?*

It was as if the lines of communication were muffled today between Jasper and me. My usual intuitive senses were confused. On one hand, he appeared to be welcoming when he asked me to walk with him and Lucas to the park. On the other hand, he never invited me up to his apartment. More than likely, I would have stayed in anyway because Jamie and I already had plans to have dinner together. But why wouldn't he accept my invitation to come over? Oh, that's right, he said he had phone calls to make. *To Who?* I couldn't help but wonder. And why did that seem more important than spending time with me? *OK, now! Stop... Just Stop!* How could I let myself think that I was the most important person in his life? Oh yeah, probably because of that electrifying kiss that's keeping me awake right now. *I'm a complete mess!*

Our attraction was undeniable, that was for sure! Our chemistry was off the charts! He obviously cared a great deal for me to come running halfway across the country to come find me in my time of distress. And every move he made after I came back to Boston made his intentions to be with me crystal clear. Up until now.

It had to be that stupid phone call! That had to be what was keeping his mind occupied. And the meaning behind it still remained a mystery to me. I was really trying to let it all go, but apparently, he wasn't. Maybe whoever it was that stole him away from me on my birthday was the same person he had to call tonight? *Oh, God! Could he be seeing someone else? I* gasped. My breath escaped me at the mere thought of it being a possibility.

Whatever the situation was... I needed more validation that I was as significant to him as he was to me, or this relationship could never work. I was already in far too deep, despite not letting on too much about it.

After tossing and turning in bed about a dozen times, seeing a new angle to my reality at every turn, I'd had enough and got up to make myself some sleepy-time tea. I hoped it might settle my mind enough to let me get some sleep. After the tea and a few chapter readings from my book, I had successfully distracted myself enough to doze off, finally… but my mind was obviously still torn.

The sunlight glistened in through the pitch pine trees that were aligning the pond as it warmly kissed my skin. My eyes caught sight of a flock of birds in the sky as they soared through the air, performing a show for me as if I were a guest in an outdoor theater.

It was quite the sight as I watched in awe. The birds dipped up and down in unison as they danced across the fluffy clouds. I flinched when one of them made a daring escape from the flock to land upon my shoulder. He was all black with sapphire undertones to his feathers and had a rolled up piece of paper stuck inside his mouth.

He quickly jumped off my shoulder and onto the bench I had been sitting on, eyeing me in a peculiar way that implored me to receive the message he was there to deliver me. Just as I began to inch closer to pull the paper from out of his mouth, he was frightened away by Lucas, who ran up to me out of nowhere, barking his head off at the flock of birds. As fast as they had swarmed in, the birds had all fled in fright.

Surely, Lucas was only trying to protect me, so I couldn't really be mad at him. When I looked up to see Jasper behind him, holding Lucas's leash, I was taken aback. Why was he wearing that mask over his face?

"Hi angel." He said, bending over to kiss me on the forehead. The sunlight dripping in from behind his silhouette nearly blinded me, but the mask was clear to see. It was crimson red and completely covered his eyes and nose, his mouth, however, I could see.

"Why are you wearing that silly mask?" I couldn't help but ask.

"What mask?" He replied with a question. His tone captured his sincere intent to his question. He truly didn't know he was wearing it. For some reason, I didn't want him to feel self conscious of it, so I let it go. The message from the bird had fallen to the ground, but I didn't want to pick it up in front of Jasper, so I left it where it lay.

Chapter 31

Tuesday morning started off as any other day would. Jamie and I had our coffee out on the patio and she left for the gym the same time I left for work. We had both agreed to send our invites out for Friday night's get together. I told her I wanted to invite Brooke and her boyfriend and she was happy to learn that I had made a new friend at work.

On my way to work, I still couldn't shake the feeling that I was being watched again. Once again, I made it to work with no major issues, besides nearly tripping over a crack in the sidewalk pavement. Embarrassed, I quickly re-balanced myself, shook it off and kept going.

When I arrived at work, Brooke had already begun our opening procedures. She had always proved to be reliable, so this was no surprise to me. I quickly dove in to help her with the side work and we caught up a bit while we still had time before we had to open the doors to the public.

"Hey, by the way, are you and Jason free on Friday night?" I asked.

"Sure. Why? Do you have something special in mind?" She asked.

"Yeah, actually...Jamie was upset that I wasn't able to properly celebrate my birthday, so we are having a little get together at our place. I would love for you and Jason to come, if you can," I said.

"Sure, that sounds like fun! I'll ask Jason and let you know for sure tomorrow. Should I bring anything?" She asked as she unlocked the door to the side entrance. As always, there were a few customers who were line up outside.

"Only if you want to. I'm sure we'll have everything we need." I replied.

The rest of the morning was pretty slow in comparison to the day before, which left Brooke and me plenty of time to catch up on everything that had transpired since I'd left for Virginia. Brooke was gushing when she heard about Jasper coming to find me.

"Wow, girl! He must really think the world of you to come halfway across the country to come find you!" she said.

"I know, I was in complete shock when he showed up at the hospital. Mama and Abby were too!" I beamed.

"So what's the deal with AJ?" She asked.

"I'm not all that sure, he was arrested, that I know do know. I gave them my statement, and Jasper said he would try to pull some strings to see if he could help him get some sort of treatment."

173

"Seriously?! After everything AJ put you through?" Brooke was baffled. "That's some next level shit, sticking his neck out for your ex... I can't wait to meet him, now! Will he be coming to the party, Friday night?" She asked, excitedly.

"I hope so, I'm gonna ask him tonight when we have dinner at his place... Wish me luck!" I laughed nervously as I remembered my plan to pour my heart out to Jasper in the card I had bought him.

When Ben arrived, I let Brooke take her break first, since she got to the shop before I did. When it was my turn to go on break, I peeked my head outside to be met with the cool crisp air from morning still loitering around and not a single cloud in the sky. There was no sign of the blonde bimbo anywhere so I took my breakfast over to the park.

The same lady was there from the night before, feeding the ducks again. Seeing her there reminded me of Jasper's remark about pulling me behind the bushes and my tummy did that flip flop thing again. *The butterflies have awoken!* I smiled to myself, as I sat there shamelessly letting my imagination run wild in fantasy land and before I knew it, my break was over.

I couldn't help but smile as the birds in the trees sang out a tune to the butterflies that happily danced within my belly. I pranced my way back to work only to find the crumbling of my smile as soon as I walked through the door.

"Blonde bimbo" was next in line to be served at the counter. *At least I thought it was her!* She looked a little shorter from what I could remember. It was difficult to tell for certain from behind and she was dressed in street clothes as opposed to that cocktail dress and heels she wore when she was making her moves on Jasper at the club.

My blood began to boil as the emotions flooded in from the memory. She appeared to be looking around the shop instead of at the tempting pastries on display right in front of her. *Was she looking for me? No, she couldn't be. How would she even know I worked here?* I was able to get a good look to confirm it was her when she turned her head to look behind her before stepping up to the counter. *Oh God! I hope she didn't spot me! I thought as* I made a dash for the bathroom to avoid being seen. I ran inside the handicapped stall and locked the door behind me. *Why on earth would she be here looking for me? I had no business with her, at all. We'd never even met!*

I sat on the toilet with my feet up for several minutes, praying she wouldn't come inside until I could no longer take the pain from holding my legs up. Since no one had entered the bathroom in the time I had been in there, I figured it was safe to come out. When I peeked around the corner, the lobby was empty and "blonde bimbo" appeared to be gone. *Phew!*

"There you are! Where have you been? You missed the rush!" Brooke asked. I stepped behind the counter and tied my apron back on.

"I'm sorry. My stomach was upset from the coffee." I lied to cover my ass. I felt bad about leaving her to deal with the workload. I wanted to tell her about everything, but I needed some time to process it in my head first.

As the day pressed on, we were pretty slow. I eventually opened up to Brooke. She was always easy to talk to. Her curious nature also seemed to make uncovering the mystery behind my drama seem fun.

It was like we were a team, deciphering all the clues, like detectives. I told her about how jealous I had gotten of "blonde bimbo" on the night that Jasper brought me home from the club. Then I confessed to her the real reason why it had taken me so long to come back from my break. I also opened up to her about feeling like I was being watched and the message I had received on the back of my car. After everything, anyone else would've thought I was crazy, but she didn't judge me at all. No, in fact, she conspired right along with me, fanning the flames to the mystery as it grew into its own twister of chaos.

"Lena!" Brooke exclaimed, somewhere in between my rambling.

"Lena?" I asked. I didn't understand why she randomly called out that name.

"Yes! That's her name!" She cried. "Your blonde bimbo, girl!"

"It is?" I asked, knowing exactly how she knew. We always wrote down our customer's name on their orders so they wouldn't get confused with the others.

"Yes! I made her coffee. In fact, she *was* acting a little suspicious! She kept looking over her shoulder the whole time she was in here." Brooke confessed. Well, at least now I had an actual name for the potential villain in my story. Brooke and I were both fascinated with the mystery behind my drama and spent the rest of the day tossing ideas back and forth between each other as the day went on until our shift ended.

~

Mama called to see how things were going on my walk home from work at the coffee shop. I wanted very much to be honest with her, but with nothing solid as to my perceived circumstances between the message on the back of my car and the blonde bimbo, Lena, I chalked it all up to my imagination having its way with me. I didn't want to cause her any unnecessary concern, so I gave her the highlights of my homecoming. I mentioned my magical date with Jasper the night I got back to Boston. I also told her about the upcoming get together for my birthday, as well as how smooth things seemed to be going with both of my jobs. Mama was more than satisfied with the crumbs I'd given her and congratulated me on the way things were going.

"It was nice talking with you." She said, "I'm so glad things are working out for you. We miss you!"

"I miss you guys too! Please tell Abby I love her. Tell her not to forget to send me pics from homecoming."

"I will, baby. Love you!" Mama said.

"Love you too, Mama! Bye!" I replied before ending the call.

When I got inside the apartment, I set my keys down on the kitchen counter and made myself a cup of sleepy time tea. I had been thinking about what I was going to say in the card to Jasper all morning and wanted to get it all down on paper. What I didn't expect was for everything to come pouring out of me like Niagara Falls. It always seemed to whenever I would sit down to write. *Why would this time would be any different?* There were things scribbled down in that notebook I was far from comfortable in sharing with Jasper just yet. I had to laugh at myself. *Thank God I chose the notebook first!*

After combing through everything I had written, I found the perfect words to express what I felt comfortable enough in saying inside the card. It was sweet, endearing and got my message across to Jasper that I was falling for him, deeply. That his attraction to me was met mutually and that I felt like the luckiest girl alive to have found him. I didn't mind telling him how I truly felt about him at all, in fact, it honestly felt freeing to let him know.

The things I didn't say in the card had far more to do with this mystery that was surrounding him and my fears of losing him to whatever that was. I didn't mention any of it because I felt extremely vulnerable to admit them. Especially since I didn't have all the facts, rather *any* for that matter, which was why I couldn't truly rely on how I felt about it. No, not until I knew more. My thirst to learn the truth was strong, but also frightening for what the outcome might actually be. I wrestled with these thoughts as I lay in bed, but with some melodic spa music I'd found online and a forceful practice of quieting my mind, I let myself drift off to sleep.

Chapter 32

I woke up feeling refreshed and decided to grab a quick shower before heading off to work at Silver Linings. Jasper had already left for the day, like usual. I couldn't help but smile when I discovered that there were still a few slices of my welcome cake left in the break room fridge. I imagined Jasper was happy to get his slice this morning.

By the time I got back home, it was 6:30 PM and I had yet to hear from Jasper, so I sent him a text message to confirm our date for dinner.

Me:

I just got in from work, are we still on for dinner tonight? My phone chimed back a minute later.

Jasper:

Change of plans

Me:

Oh, really? My heart sank deep into my chest. I had been looking forward to our date all day long. *Was he really going to cancel out on me at the last minute?*

Jasper:

We're going out instead. It's my buddy, Sam's birthday. I'm sorry Angel. I just couldn't tell him no. Can you meet me upstairs in 30 minutes? You can get ready here. I had your dress dry cleaned, by the way... it's perfect for where we're going.

Me:

Oh... really? Okay. That sounds nice. I'll see you then!

How could I have forgotten about my dress? It was emerald green with a split clean up to my hip on the side and had a sheer layer of iridescent shimmer material that covered the entire dress. The spaghetti straps accentuated my cleavage and was cut low enough in the back to meet my waist length auburn hair when it was down. In it's provocative form, I felt a little self conscious when I wore it, but it had been confirmed by enough people that I was able to pull it off very well.

Obviously Jasper liked the way I appeared in it, if he wanted me to wear it again. It had gotten soaked from the rain the night Jasper took me home from Club Hush. I remembered it all too well in detail. My stomach took a dive at the mere memory of that night. I had finally found validation in the power behind our mutual attraction to one another. I was downright crazy for him that night.

I had never been comfortable enough to dance alone the way I did that night to allure Jasper to me. My plan worked like a charm. So well, that Jasper not only met me out on the dance floor but also rescued me from a situation I truly wanted out of with Eddie.

Eddie, who coincidentally turned out to be Jamie's new boyfriend, Dillon's best friend, had his sights on me the first time I had gone to Club Hush with Jamie and her friends. He nearly brawled with Jasper to keep me the night Jasper wound up taking me home. Jasper showed me the strength of his maturity when he quickly swept me away and took me home in his SUV, rather than giving into the whims of an alcohol induced quest to polish Eddie's ego.

I found the mirrored wedge sandals I had purchased to go with the dress that Jamie bought me for my birthday. They were sitting on the floor of the closet in my bedroom. At least, now I wouldn't have to decide on what to wear for dinner on such short notice. Whether he knew how special they were to me or not, these little things Jasper did for me never went unnoticed and continued to strengthen my attraction to him,

The idea of meeting Sam, Jasper's business partner, had me both excited and nervous. I didn't ask Jasper where we were going because I wanted it to be a surprise. The fact that I didn't have to worry about deciding what to wear made it much easier to relax about how I might come across to the co-owner of Club Hush.

A few minutes after texting with Jasper, Jamie walked through the front door with a bag of Chinese takeout. I had already told her of my plans with Jasper for dinner so she was already expecting me to be gone for the night.

"Hey. Smells good, what'd ya get?" I asked as I watched her take her shoes off.

"My usual. Honey Garlic Chicken, fried rice and wanton soup." She replied.

"Yum, sounds good." I said. I stole the bonus fortune cookie out of the bag she had set down on the kitchen counter.

"So... I think Brooke and her boyfriend, Jason, will be coming on Friday. She's gonna get back to me tomorrow for sure. Oh, and guess what? We're meeting Jasper's friend, Sam, tonight for dinner."

"Really?" She asked with a raise of her eyebrows. "I thought you guys were having dinner at his place?"

"That was the original plan, but apparently it's his birthday, and he couldn't turn down his invitation." I replied.

"Where are you guys going?" She asked.

"I'm not sure, but he told me to wear that dress you bought me. He had it dry cleaned. I guess I'll be getting ready at his place. I'm gonna grab a quick shower before I go. I need to meet him upstairs in like 20 minutes!"

"You'd better hurry then! Go! You don't wanna keep him waiting too long." Jamie laughed as I crunched down on my fortune cookie. *Mmm...* Fresh and crispy, just the way I liked them. I pinned the fortune under a magnet on the fridge for later reading and ran to get ready.

Chapter 33

W hen I walked inside Jasper's apartment, he was sitting on the couch waiting for me. There were 2 glasses of red wine sitting on the coffee table. Lucas was likely upstairs in his crate, because he didn't come rushing at me like he always seemed to do.

"Hey you! Come sit down for a minute." Jasper said. His masculine tone was alluring, not that he needed any help in bringing me towards him. My body naturally wanted to gravitate towards him all the time, despite whatever nonsense might have been going on inside my head.

"Hey. How are you?" I smiled shyly as I sat down a few feet away from him. "Is this for me?" I boldly asked as I reached for one of the glasses on the coffee table.

"Of course. Since we're having a late dinner, I thought we might relax for a little bit before we get ready. You don't mind the change in our plans, do you?"

"Not at all, I had the best time the last time we went out!" I said, recalling the amazing Greek restaurant he had taken me to. "By the way, do you remember the party we were supposed to have for my birthday?" I asked, shyly.

"You mean the one that never happened? Yes. Is it being rescheduled?" He asked, with a raise of his eyebrows.

"Yes, actually... Jamie wants to reschedule it for Friday. Do you think you can make it?" I asked.

"Absolutely. You know I wouldn't miss it for the world, Angel. I really hope you like the place we're going to tonight." He said, eyeing me hungrily as he inched closer to me on the sofa. My temperature rose in a blush to my cheeks and my heart rate quickened. "So...How was your day?" His voice took on a seductive tone.

"Not bad," My skin felt flushed and I wondered if he could tell how flustered I was. I nervously fumbled around with my wine glass, feeling the texture beneath my fingers as I took a generous gulp into my mouth. I had hoped the wine might settle my nerves. *Why does my body react this way any time he comes near me?* I had to wonder as I let my eyes roam over to a stack of magazines that were sitting on the coffee table. I nearly died when he splayed his hand across my lap. There was no hiding it now, for sure.

"Angel?" He asked, with a gentle tug at my chin, drawing my attention to his face. We locked eyes, and I knew it was clear just how much I had been anticipating his kiss.

"Come here." He said, putting his lips on mine.

I was so captivated by my own nerves, I hadn't distinguished the fact that Jasper was already spirited by the wine. And I was just as intoxicated, only it wasn't because of the wine. I was channeled in to the scent of his cologne and his natural pheromones. My breath hitched and my eyes squinted at the halo glow that seemed to be forming all around us. It was as if every inch of my skin was on high alert. I couldn't help but wonder if maybe I was dreaming. Dreaming or not, I was enjoying every lust filled second, despite my body's unease. He was like a drug and I was dangerously drawn. My body instinctively leaned into his kiss when he pulled me into his arms. The heat between us, blazing hot, like wildfire. I could feel his own enchantment in the exchange of energy in our kiss. As things began to escalate rapidly between us, I knew it wouldn't be long before we both stripped down to nothing right there on his couch! I didn't want to forget to give him the card and gift before I lost my nerve.

"Wait! I have something for you." I blurted out, breaking away from his embrace. Jasper looked confused. I knew that once I said it, there would be no turning back. I stood up from the couch to grab my bag from off the kitchen island and presented Jasper with the card, first. "This is for you, but I don't want you to open it in front of me." I said, before modestly handing him the gift. "And this... this is for Lucas. You can open that now."

"Alright... Let's see what it is, then." He said. He slowly peeled away the wrapping paper with every intent to playfully mock me. When he finally revealed the rubber hot dog toy inside, his entire face lit up. I could honestly revel in this moment forever, the way the light flickered in his sapphire blue eyes. "It's a hot dog!" He laughed.

"Yes!" I laughed. "One that he can keep forever!"

"I love it! And I know he will too!" Jasper said, pulling me in for a kiss.

When we heard Lucas whining from upstairs, it was honestly a welcoming distraction. We both knew that there was no time for us to get down to business and still be on time for dinner.

"Damn it! I guess I better take him out before we leave. Damn mutt!" We both laughed.

"Yeah, that's probably a good idea." I said.

"You can get ready while I'm gone. Your dress is hanging in my closet upstairs."

"Okay." I agreed.

I followed Jasper up the stairs to his loft, where he let Lucas out of his crate. Lucas came charging up to me, like always. Jasper quickly grabbed a hold of his leash and held it up in the air to get a grasp on Lucas's attention.

"C'mon boy, you wanna go out?" He asked. Lucas wagged his little nub in excitement.

"Feel free to use the bathroom upstairs, if you'd like." Jasper said to me as he fastened the leash onto Lucas's collar.

"Okay. Have fun, you two!" I replied.

"We'll be back in a bit." Jasper called out as they both fumbled their way down the stairs.

I found my dress hanging in Jasper's closet next to his suits and ties. I had to admit, I was tempted to snoop around a little. I fought the urge and pulled my dress down from the hanger and brought it with me into the bathroom to get ready.

I got dressed, refreshed my hair and makeup and went downstairs to wait for Jasper and Lucas to return. I wasn't waiting very long when they came rushing through the penthouse. Lucas was full of energy, dragging Jasper behind him, leading me to wonder who was walking who in that scenario.

"I'm gonna bring Lucas upstairs and get ready. I'll be down in a few minutes. There's more wine on the bar in the kitchen if you'd like." Jasper said with a quick peck to my lips.

~

Jasper turned the soft jazz music up on our drive to the restaurant. It almost seemed as if it were a deterrence to distract me from his quiet and pensive demeanor. It was always a thrill to be in close proximity of Jasper within the confines of the soft leather interior of his SUV. The air between us was filled with the alluring scent of his cologne, but his energy was still a bit off.

After riding in the music filled silence, I reached my hand across to him to see if I could detect anything specific in his touch. A bit surprised by my advance, he flinched ever so slightly before taking my hand in his and brushing the pad of his thumb over the underside of my wrist.

When we arrived at the restaurant, I was surprised that they had valet service for parking. I had never been to a restaurant with valet service before, so it was all new to me. I began to feel a bit nervous that I hadn't a clue on how to act when it came to proper fine dining etiquette. The valet serviceman opened my door for me and I stepped out into a well lit circular driveway. Jasper quickly stepped in behind me, placing the palm of his hand at the small of my back to guide me down a path to the grand entrance of the building. I was in awe as we passed several beautiful sculpted fountains accentuated by multi-colored lights on each side of the path we walked down. We were greeted by a doorman wearing a 3 piece suit.

"We have a reservation for four under Sam." Jasper said to the doorman.

"Yes, sir. Right this way. We hope your experience is pleasurable." The gentleman replied as he opened the door and handed us off to a gorgeous blonde woman. She looked like she belonged on the cover of a magazine. She was beautifully dressed in a long fitted royal blue mermaid styled gown that emphasized her perfect figure and the sway of her well rounded hips.

"Good evening Mr. Sullivan, madame." She said with a nod in my direction. "Please follow me to your table, your party is waiting for you."

We walked down a long hallway that appeared to be charmed by historical romance era oil paintings. Deep burgundy and golden hued tones were prominent in the marbled flooring. I was easily enchanted by my surroundings as I swiftly cast my suspicions about Jasper's manner on our drive up here to the back burner of my mind. *How could I not be fascinated by everything I saw around me?* I'd never been to a place so fancy before.

When we arrived at our table, my trance was quickly stolen away by a pair of dark brown eyes staring back at me. Her blonde hair and icy fair complexion was one I wished I had soon forgotten. I couldn't believe my eyes! Lena, the blonde bimbo, was seated at our table next to Jasper's business partner, Sam. *She was his date!* I gasped, uncontrollably. Sam was attractive. He had short, golden brown hair that he wore slicked back and matching golden brown eyes. His skin was tanned, as if he made a regular habit of spending leisure time out in the sun.

"Are you alright?" Jasper asked me in a whisper as he pulled my chair out for me to take a seat.

"Yeah, I'm good." I whispered back as I politely greeted the couple. "Hello, I'm Carla." I said, raising my hand in a friendly wave to the pair as I hid behind a mask of false confidence. They both smiled and greeted me back. I don't know what it was, but there was definitely something dark I was sensing from their energy. An air of mischief I couldn't seem to put my finger on, but it was all right there, lurking beneath the surface. Jasper settled himself into the chair next to mine and I quickly reminded myself to focus on my etiquette. I took a deep breath, hoping to swallow whatever it was that I was feeling and placed my cloth napkin inside my lap.

"Carla, this is Sam, my best friend and business partner, and his girlfriend Lena." Jasper said, quickly filling the space with the warmth I needed to settle my nerves that began to rapidly rise to the surface.

"Hi!" Sam said warmly, as he extended his hand out to shake mine. Lena followed suit, but didn't say a word. Her handshake only confirmed the reason why my radar was on such high alert with her. She felt as cold as her eyes in terms of character and barely had any strength in the grip of her handshake. *Was she hiding something? She couldn't possibly know how perceptive I was in reading people's energy, could she? I wondered.*

"Pleasure to meet you both." I said in their direction.

"We ordered some hors d'oeuvres. Would you care for a glass of wine?" Sam offered me.

The table had been set with 2 different types of stemware at each of our place settings. Several pieces of silverware lay properly at each side of the stack of various sizes of plates. I was beginning to feel overwhelmed by what was in front of me. It reminded me of that scene in Pretty Woman when Julia Roberts didn't know which fork to use. I felt so out of place.

"Yes, please." I said, welcoming a chance for some liquid courage to make it through this dinner without making a complete ass out of myself. Sam poured wine into one of my empty glasses.

"Jasper?" He asked.

"No, thank you." he replied. I was clueless as to what I had walked into here, but the tension between them seemed very high, I could literally cut it with a knife.

"I'll have a Scotch on the rocks. Can you make it a double, please?" Jasper asked the waiter when he came to the table with a basket of fresh baked bread and several mouth watering appetizers. Ahh, finally something I was more than comfortable with-food!

"Of course, sir. May I present Fried Calamari with Cocktail and Lemon, Mussels Marinara and Crispy Fried Zucchini. Please enjoy! I'll be back to take your order in a few minutes." The waiter said with a small wink in my direction and a very welcoming smile to follow. *Ahh... Finally! Someone I could get a good read on!*

"Thank you. It looks delicious!" Sam said to the waiter when all the plates were settled on the table in front of us. "I've been trying to reach you all week...Where have you been?" Sam asked Jasper in the waiter's departure.

"I know, I'm sorry. I've uh... been busy working on a project. You know I wouldn't miss your birthday, brother." Jasper replied in a cautious tone.

"Well, I'm glad you could make it tonight, at least." Sam said as he poured the last of the wine in the bottle into Lena's glass.

"Thank you, Sam." She said, her Russian accent shining prominently through her words. I watched as she carelessly brought the glass to her lips while darting a glance in Jasper's direction. I shifted in my chair to mask losing control of my nerves. Jasper cleared his throat as if he were going to say something, but remained silent, instead.

"I have some exciting news I wanted to share with you. Well, *we* want to share with you." Sam said, pulling Lena closer into his side as he flashed her a giant sparkle-toothed smile. He was clearly in love with her. It was difficult to tell, however, if she saw him in that same light. "Lena's pregnant! We're gonna have a baby." Sam seemed genuinely excited, the initial expression on Lena's face seemed... callous? Until she offered her boyfriend an obviously fake smile in return. At least, that was my interpretation, anyway. But I tried to give her the benefit of doubt. After all, I was just meeting these two for the first time. My sense of intuition could have been off.

"That is exciting. I'm happy for the two of you." Jasper said, with a clench of his jaw. It was a tell tale sign that he was biting his tongue on something. I had seen it the night of the club when he fought the urge to fight with Eddie on the dance floor. I was delighted to hear that Lena would no longer be any sort of threat to my relationship, as I had once suspected. I just couldn't seem to shake this feeling like I was a fly on the wall throughout this entire conversation. It honestly felt like there were things being left unsaid on both sides of the spectrum, which led me to wonder what the hell was going on. I could feel the tension radiating off of Jasper. He was definitely angry about something.

"You sure that's a good idea?" Jasper finally bit out, gesturing to the wine in Lena's glass.

"It's fine. Apparently, the doctor told Lena a glass or two a day would do no harm." Sam said as though he was fully confident in her admission.

"Is that so?" Jasper asked, with an icy glare in Lena's direction. "Would you all please excuse me. I need to use the restroom." Jasper said before nodding at us all and getting up from the table. I watched as he took the glass of scotch he had ordered off the tray that was making its way over to our table when he walked away. With so many questions running through my mind, I couldn't help myself from stalking Jasper's every move. With his back to me, I couldn't actually see him drink the entire glass, but when he set the empty glass on the bar before turning a corner, it was a clear indication that he had finished it.

"And for you, Miss?" I was quickly drawn back to the reality in front of me when the waiter tried to take my order. *Earth to Carla!*

"I'm sorry, would you mind if I took a few more minutes to look over the menu?" I asked, politely.

"Absolutely, madame. Take all the time you need." The waiter replied before leaving our table.

"Would you please excuse me?" I asked in Sam's direction. He replied with a shrug. I refused to let my eyes meet Lena's again. I placed my napkin on the table and stood up from my chair to escape my unease. I needed to get some air. This was all too much for me! I was surprised when I found Jasper sitting on the ledge that surrounded the bushes at the front entrance. "Hey." I said. He turned around to look into my eyes and I could see a storm brewing inside them. This was a side I had yet to see from him before. "Are you alright?" I asked.

"I'm fine. I just needed to get some air. It was a little too stuffy inside." He replied, his eyes softening as he studied the concern on my face.

"Well, can I ask what the hell all that was about back there?" I dared myself to ask, quickly feeling the sting of regret the moment I let the words pass my lips.

"It's a long story. I would rather not talk about it right now." Jasper replied. Clearly his state of mind was more consuming than his ability to take notice of how bold I had been in asking.

"Okay, well... What are we supposed to be doing right now? Aren't we here for your friend's birthday?" I asked. I was so confused.

"Yes. We probably should go back inside, but I would honestly prefer not to." He wasn't making any sense. I could tell that something was bothering him, but it was clear he wasn't ready to talk about it.

"I don't understand. Do you want me to tell them that we're leaving?" The truth was, I was completely onboard with getting the hell out of dodge on this beautifully, exquisite disaster of a dinner date.

"No." He replied. "You know what? Yes. If you don't mind. Just tell them I'm not feeling very well. I'll ask the valet to bring the car."

"Okay. I'll be back in a few minutes." I wasn't going to ask any more questions.

"Wait!" Jasper called out to stop me from going back inside. He reached into his jacket pocket for his wallet and handed me his AMEX card. "Please give this to the hostess and tell her to run my card for the bill. Wish Sam a Happy Birthday for me and tell them to order anything they'd like. Dinner is on me." I was more confused than ever now, but didn't know what else to do besides agree to his request. "Okay."

He placed both hands on each of my shoulders. "Thanks Angel. We'll get something for dinner on the way home, I promise." By now, my appetite was already gone. Having dinner was the furthest thing from my mind. But I could see in his eyes just much he needed me right now and the last thing I wanted to do was let him down.

"Of course." I said, reassuring him with a smile before turning to go back inside the restaurant to fulfill his request.

Chapter 34

Jasper

I knew this night was going to be hard. I couldn't help but to waver in faith that somehow the outcome might change. The audacity she had to sit there, right in front of me, drinking her Goddamn wine in my face right after I spent my entire morning trying to talk her out of an abortion was just unheard of! Then again, I always knew that she was evil. I felt it in my bones the moment I met her.

She knew damn well that doctor didn't tell her it was OK for her to drink! I knew because I was sitting right next to her when he told her she needed to stop. Hell, I'd even went as far as writing that $2 million fucking dollar check she asked me for to keep her from going through with it. Whether I was actually going to give it to her now was an entirely different story.

I should have known that bringing Carla with me tonight was a huge mistake. A mistake that was sure to strip her away from me. *Fuck! How could I be so careless with her?* I just really needed her, here with me... She was the only thing in this world that brought me any peace, the only person in my life that actually made sense! And now, I hadn't the slightest clue as to what I could do to keep her.

What was worse was the fact that I still didn't know how I ended up in bed with Lena that night in the first fucking place or how I had let myself get so drunk. That whole night was a blur.

My days of drinking more than 2 or 3 drinks in a night were long over, years ago. I traded it for keeping everything under control at all times. A lesson I'd learned after a huge blow up over nothing with Sam when we were both young and stupid. I can't even recall what we were fighting about, but I remembered how it landed him in the hospital with a broken arm. We laughed about it afterwards, but I still felt guilty every time I watched him reach inside his cast to scratch the uncontrollable itch it came with.

Still, the fact remained that there was a baby that would soon be born into this world, and whether it was mine or Sam's, it was still hers. Knowing she had complete control over what would happen with this baby was slowly eating me alive.

Carla

The ride back was filled with more silence, only this time the music was lacking. Jasper seemed to be lost in his own world. He barely even noticed when I turned the radio up slightly for my own sanity. I needed to quiet my own mind, somehow, after everything that went down inside the restaurant.

The only words exchanged between us had been when he asked me if

I was okay with Chicken Parmesan for dinner and when he placed the order for delivery on his cell phone. My eyes were fixated on the city lights as I let the music fill the space between my ears. The traffic lights all seemed to pass us by at what felt like lightning speed. After a quick glance over at the speedometer I had confirmed that we were moving nearly 20 miles over the posted limit. I wasn't the slightest bit afraid at all, as Jasper seemed to have complete control of the vehicle we were in and there was hardly any traffic. It honestly felt exhilarating and only enhanced the thrill of being within close proximity to him despite whatever turmoil had been shifting back and forth inside the space of my mind. For a moment, I had almost completely forgotten about the shit show we had both just escaped. That didn't change the fact that there were so many questions I wanted answers for. *Why was he so triggered by this woman I had finally discovered a name for other than "blonde bimbo"? What did Lena have on him?* Clearly, it was something of extreme importance! *And why on earth would he leave his best friend's birthday dinner after he revealed something so life changing as having a baby on the way? Why wouldn't he be happy for his friend?*

The Jasper I knew would have wanted to celebrate this milestone with someone he claimed was his best friend. I knew that without a single shred of doubt. Then again, the man sitting next to me was far from being himself right now either. In no other circumstance before this, had he ever let me do his dirty work of telling *his* friends he wasn't coming back to the table. Not that I minded. I was more than happy to take the reins if it meant bringing him some peace. Relationships were a place for give and take and I couldn't always be sitting on the receiving end. That wouldn't be fair to either of us.

Still, this was not the protective Jasper I knew at all. No, this man was in a completely different mode. A reclusive mode of self preservation.

This was his other side he had yet to reveal to me. And even though I didn't like seeing him in this light or the fact that he was clearly tormented by it, it made me feel closer to him than ever before.

The reasons for my own discomfort at that table may have been entirely different from his, or perhaps they were one in the same? Only time would reveal the answers I sought. I was hoping that eventually, Jasper would, himself. One way or the other, I was going to find out. Regardless of what those answers might be, I could not escape how deeply I had fallen for this man who sat beside me. There was no denying how magnetically drawn to him I was. That was more than evident now in the constant energy that surrounded us. This attraction, I truly believed, may have been what drew me all the way to Boston in the first place. It was almost as if I were sirenned to him by the divine. *Perhaps it was him who had called out for me?*

Even back home, the signs were all there. They'd been following me all along! *How could I not notice them?* Not only were they lying beneath every dark cloud I was surrounded by, I could feel them in my every move. It was what had kept me alive in the darkness that had seemingly consumed me. It was the spark that kept me going, day after lonesome day. I had hope for a better life. I had hope that true love existed and that it would one day find me. It shimmied its way through in every smile I exchanged with the people around me.

Chapter 35

W hen we arrived back at the apartment, Jasper opened the car door for me, just the same as he always did. A sign that even in his brooding, he was still capable of chivalry. He followed close behind me with his hand pressed firmly against my back as we walked through the parking garage, then opened the door to the lobby to let me in before him.

Upon our entrance into the lobby, we saw the delivery boy from the pizza place I had grown to love. He was speaking to Freddie, the security guard, holding a large brown paper bag.

"That must be our dinner." Jasper said to me as we approached the security desk. "Is that for me?" Jasper asked the pair of gentlemen who were standing before us.

"Yes. Yes, it is." Freddie replied to Jasper.

"Okay, thank you. I'll take it from here." Jasper said as he reached inside his jacket pocket for his wallet. He handed the delivery driver a hundred dollar bill. The driver started to reach into his pocket when he was quickly halted by Jasper's hand. "Don't worry about it, the change is for you." He said as he took the bag from the driver's hand.

"Oh, wow! Thank you sir!" The driver said to Jasper before darting out the front door entrance of the lobby. It seemed as though he was afraid Jasper might change his mind.

When the elevator door closed behind us, the aroma of olive oil and garlic invoked my spirit of hunger like magic, as it always did. My biological father, John was a full blooded Italian. He inherently left me with genetics that would never let me miss a great Italian meal. I could tell Jasper was still silently brooding, but once we got inside his penthouse, he finally broke our marathon of silence.

"I'm truly sorry about tonight, Angel." Jasper said, daring himself to look me in the eye as he placed the bag containing our dinner on the counter of the kitchen island. "I never should have put you in the middle of all that I have going on right now. I'm sure you have a million questions. Honestly, I wish I could answer them all for you, but I just need some time to think." He peered into my eyes and took my hands in his. "So for now, if you don't mind… can we please have a nice dinner and put everything else beside us for the night. Perhaps we can just enjoy each other's company?" It wasn't an unbearable request. I knew he wasn't ready to open up to me, and if there was anyone in this world who could understand that, it was me. Even though he was right, many questions were haunting me in terms of where we stood with each other among this crazy, mysterious drama that appeared to be unfolding in his world.

I also felt like his heart was ultimately in the right place when it came to me. I wanted nothing more than to hold on to what we had and bring each other comfort over everything else. The truth was, I needed him just as much as he needed me.

"Of course!" I said, warmly. "Besides, I think whatever you got in that bag deserves our attention, anyway, Don't you think? It smells fantastic! Are you hungry?" I asked, lending him a smile that softened the tension between us with ease. His reactive smirk in return was all I really needed in that moment, anyway. That and the return of his one-cheeked dimple.

"Starved! In more ways than one, Angel. You have no idea!" Jasper replied with a sharp exhale as he replaced his sweet smile with one that was laced with mischief. He reached over my shoulder to open the cabinet and take down some plates for us to dish out our dinner. It was everything the aroma had claimed it to be.

By the time we finished eating, Jasper and I were both so full, we could barely move. I helped him clean up from dinner and we both settled onto the couch to watch some TV. Eventually, Law and Order lost our interest. I had seen the show on the screen so many times before, I could almost quote it verbatim.

When Jasper began caressing my arm, I knew my plans of getting home early were all out the window. There was something so magical about his touch I just couldn't resist. It would've taken everything I had inside me to resist his lips when he pressed them into mine, and frankly, I had no intention of denying him in the first place. He flicked off the remote control and led me upstairs.

When we reached the top of the loft, Lucas cried out in excitement.

Jasper let him out of his crate.

"I need to take him out. Do you wanna come with me? Or would you prefer to stay here and relax?" Jasper asked.

"I'll come with you, if that's okay? I wouldn't mind walking off that dinner anyway." I replied, momentarily forgetting the fact that I didn't bring my sneakers with me. Jasper took Lucas's leash from off the table and hooked it on to Lucas's collar and we all made quite the spectacle of our journey down the stairs. Jasper pushed the button for the elevator and we all piled inside.

When we got downstairs, Freddie was ending his shift for the night and a new guard, one I'd never seen before, was taking over for the night.

"I didn't forget about what you asked me, Miss." Freddie said to me. *Shit!* "I'm still waiting for my boss to get back to me. He said we would need to file a police report if we found anything." Jasper raised his eyebrows in my direction as he struggled to keep Lucas from rushing out the door to the front entrance. I swear it took all his strength to pull Lucas back over to the front desk where I was still standing with Freddie.

"What's this all about?" Jasper wasted no time in asking with a look of concern dredged across his face.

"Okay, that won't be necessary. Don't worry about it. Thank you, Freddie." I said to Freddie. I didn't want to keep him there any longer than he needed to be, especially since I was well aware that I didn't want to go as far as filing yet another police report. Lord knew, I'd already had enough drama with law enforcement for the month.

"It's nothing. Please don't worry about it." I replied to Jasper with an expression that pleaded with him not to dig.

"You sure? It sure doesn't sound like nothing." He said, as he begrudgingly gave in to my silent plea to not ask questions. The clench in his jaw was a clear indication of how much he struggled to bite his tongue. With everything that had gone on previously in the evening, he knew he didn't have a leg to stand on in terms of demanding an answer from me. Without his own admissions, he knew his hands were tied. The only option he really had was to simply respect my decision to keep the issue private.

We walked in silence, mostly. Thankfully, Lucas was quick to finish his business as both my feet and the silence between us were killing me.

"Look. I know you want me to tell you about what Freddie and I spoke of, but I just don't feel that the timing is right to put anything more on your plate, right now." I said as we approached the apartment building. "Surely you've got quite a bit going on, the last thing you need is to worry about me, especially when it really is nothing to worry about." I said, in hopes of easing some of the tension.

"I just want to make sure you're safe, Angel. That's all I really care about. Promise me that if you ever feel you are in any sort of danger, you won't keep me in the dark about it, please" Jasper said as he opened the door to let us inside the building. *Is omitting the truth really lying? Hadn't I learned this already by what had happened with Abby?* I questioned myself before responding. Regardless of the lesson I'd recently learned, my instincts were telling me otherwise. I needed to make him feel that I was in no part in harm's way. That's not to say that his protective nature hadn't instantly dove in to retrieve the butterflies as they all came fluttering to the surface. They always had a way of reminding me of how insanely attracted to this man I really was.

"I promise. I will come to you if I ever feel that I'm in any sort of danger." I said beneath my lashes. My eyes were filled with enough lust to sidetrack his brain as we stepped inside the elevator. "I wasn't planning on staying over tonight because I have to work early in the morning, but would you mind if I did?" I asked, boldly stepping out of my comfort zone. *Who even am I right now?* I had to ask myself. Surely I was possessed by the spellbound energy I seemed to be in. The truth was, I would walk on fire to bridge the gap between us. And if I could bring the heat with me, perhaps we could both, at the very least, settle our desire for one another before the night was over.

"I told you, Angel. I would never deny you. Of course you can. I just hope I can be of good company, it's been a rough night."

"Even if we just watch TV, I would be more than fine with that. I just can't be late for work in the morning. Can you make sure I am up in time to go downstairs and get ready?" I asked.

"Of course. I have to be up early tomorrow anyway, I have an important meeting after work and I want to make sure everything is tended to at the office." Jasper replied.

When we got upstairs, we went straight up to the loft and got ready to watch some TV in bed. Jasper gave me a t-shirt to sleep in and I shot a text out to Jamie to let her know I would be staying at Jasper's for the night.

I felt so cozy wrapped up in Jasper's arms beneath his goose down comforter. Somehow, between the lull of the TV and the comfort of Jasper's warm body pressed into mine as I listened to the beat of his heart, I was able to quiet the many questions still running through my mind. Sam's birthday dinner only deepened the mystery of this drama surrounding Jasper's world. It also exhausted me to a point where I was quick to fall asleep the moment my body felt comfortable.

~

I didn't want to disturb her. Somehow, in her sleep, she was even more beautiful than ever. *My Angel.* Just the sight of her and feeling her close to me kept me sane, but the last thing my mind wanted to do right now was sleep. I felt so guilty for keeping this secret from her, knowing well enough she needed me to come clean about everything.

My biggest problem was, I had no idea how I would approach this situation with her without making her run for the hills. She still had a long way to go in terms of healing from everything she'd been through with AJ. Anyone who truly cared about her would see that. I honestly thought having me by her side to protect her through it all would have been what was best for her. Until I got that stupid phone call that ruined everything we were working towards in our relationship.

The plate she was carrying was heavy enough without my own burdens on top. I just knew that if I came clean about the possibility that I might become a father soon was sure to scare her off. Add the fact that the mother of my first and only child could possibly be my own best friend's girlfriend. I just knew it wouldn't sit right with her. Hell, it damn sure didn't sit right with me, and I was the guilty party in all of this.

I still couldn't seem to wrap my head around the fact that I somehow managed to wind up in bed with her. The crazy part was that I didn't even know how I got there in the first place. I always had my suspicions about Lena, from the time that I met her. Something about her just never sat right with me. I never felt like I could trust her. The way she callously made my best friend feel like the happiest man alive, all while slithering her wandering eyes in my direction had completely turned me off. It wasn't even the fact that she seemed to be more interested in me than she was in Sam, if I was being completely honest. It was more in the fact that she had no conscience about the spell she had him under and what she was doing to my best friend. Whether she cared about Sam or not, I did. He was my best friend, for Christ's sake. I could never do anything that would bring him any harm. It just wasn't in my nature, regardless of my tumultuous past of having been with so many women.

When Carla came into my life, I knew she was the one for me. I felt it in my soul when I looked into her Angel eyes. Somehow, with her presence, my life had actually felt like it had meaning for the very first time. I had someone to love. Someone who would love me in a way I had always longed for. Even when she wasn't ready, I still felt in my bones that she was sent to save me from the life I was meandering about with no true fulfillment.

Sure, I had my moments, when I would give back to the community by volunteering my free time, but somehow it never seemed like it was fulfilling enough to satisfy me. No matter how much of my time I gave, I kept feeling the need to give more.

These thoughts were so loud in my head, I knew I would never get to sleep. I carefully wriggled myself free from Carla without waking her and got out of bed for a glass of milk, hoping it might help me sleep. Tomorrow was a big day. I had to meet with the contractors I was hiring to do some work for the property I had just purchased. I needed to get some rest, so I had to at least try.

When I made my way into the kitchen, I noticed the card that Carla brought me sitting on the island counter. I remembered her asking me to read it when she wasn't around. I couldn't understand why, other than the fact that she may have felt embarrassed or shy about whatever she wrote inside the card. Since she was upstairs, and technically sleeping, I let my curiosity for what was inside the card take over. I need to distract my mind anyway. Perhaps her words might bring me some comfort and let me find my way to some much needed rest. I poured myself a glass of milk and sat down on the stool to read the card.

Dear Jasper,

In a world of darkness you shined your light.
    The flicker of flame I held onto
    you somehow found a way to ignite.
    I get lost in the magic of your touch.
    And can't help but wonder how I can feel so much
    In so little time.
    The passion between us took me by surprise.
    A home I have found when I look in your eyes.
    How did I ever get so lucky?
    To have you here with me?
    And you call me your angel,

but with you, that's all that I see.

I wanted to take the time to say thank you for being the one sure thing in my life. Everything is moving so fast, but with you, it feels like time stands still. Your kind and caring nature nurtures my soul and makes me feel so warm and peaceful. And though, at times, I feel like I'm out on a limb, I just know you would never let me fall. I feel it instinctively. Even though this is all new territory for me, I wanted you to know that with you, I feel safe and protected, always. I felt it that first day when we met at the park and that feeling has never left me.

I have never been one to speak of my true emotions. Any time I try, I'm an incoherent mess! It always comes out better on paper. Knowing that about myself, I wanted you to know how I truly felt in the best way I know how because I know I won't ever come right out and say it in person. I can only hope that you feel it in my energy whenever I am with you.

With Love,

Carla

I was surprised that she had taken up nearly every inch of space in the card that wasn't already used by the greeting. No wonder why she felt shy to have me read it in front of her. Her beautiful handwriting and how well it was written did not surprise me one bit. Everything about her was astonishing to me. The meaning behind her words tugged at my heart like no one else had before. I only wished she felt more comfortable in sharing how she felt with me. I would never judge her for sharing her feelings, it was what I truly wanted.

The funny thing is, nearly everything she'd written had already been gifted to me whenever I looked into those beautiful angelic brown eyes of hers. The truth was, I did everything she had poured out to me in that card in the energy that surrounded us whenever we were together.

Her heart is what drew me to her in the first place. I admired her authenticity and how tightly she held on to it, whether she realized it or not. Even though my mind was still tormented by everything that had come to light between Lena and Sam and this baby, seeing everything here in black and white was only confirmation of everything I had felt from the moment I laid eyes on Carla.

The validation of her words did seem to help release a little of the tension I was feeling. It also made me realize just how special our connection was and that I had to do everything in my power to protect it. Even if that meant separating myself from her so I could think everything through with a clear head. I especially knew I needed to keep her at bay during this time. The last thing I wanted was for her to pick up on the energy of the turmoil I was facing. She'd been through enough.

With her heartfelt words tucked into my heart, I went back upstairs to crawl in bed next to her. I took in her scent and rested on the decision that I would have to let her know I would be leaving tomorrow. It wouldn't come easy, and I could only pray she might understand my reasons why.

Chapter 36

Carla

The alarm on my phone had served its purpose in waking me up at 5 AM. I rolled over in bed to find that I was not in my own. Although I felt very well rested, somehow, I had completely forgotten that I had decided to stay the night over at Jasper's place. He wasn't here in bed with me though.

Apparently he went to take Lucas out for a walk since they both seemed to be gone when I went downstairs to find him. The smell of freshly brewed coffee allured me into the kitchen in search of a mug. It wasn't but a few minutes after I made my coffee that I heard the ding of the elevator and Jasper and Lucas flooded inside the penthouse.

"Good morning, Angel. How did you sleep?" Jasper asked me. The sweat on his t-shirt accentuated his broad chest and strong arms. I couldn't help myself from comparing him to AJ, who's sweat had always been so heavily saturated with alcohol that the off putting smell repulsed me. But with Jasper, this was not the case at all! Seeing him all hot and sweaty from his run released endorphins inside me that made me want him even more. I found myself working over time to shake my wayward thoughts away to manage my composure.

"I think I slept a little too well." I replied with a giggle. "I completely forgot where I was when I woke up. I hope you don't mind that I helped myself to some coffee." I said as I inhaled the steam from my mug.

"Not at all. I made it for you." He said as he released Lucas from his leash, who in turn came right up to me with his little nub of a tail wagging like it was nobody's business. I reached down to give him a pat on the head.

"Good morning, Lucas." I cried out in a squeaky voice. "Did you have fun on your walk?" Lucas shrugged his eyebrows and gave my hand a giant lick. Jasper sat down on the bar stool next to me with his own cup of coffee and gave me a sweet kiss on my forehead. My body tingled at his touch. *Ahh, I could get used to this!*

"So…" Jasper sighed. "I have something I want to talk with you about." *OMG! Was he actually going to open up to me about everything that went on last night? I'm barely even awake yet!* I braced myself and wondered whether I would actually have enough time to hear him out. I really needed to get my butt downstairs to get ready for work!

"Is that so?" I asked in a cautious tone.

"Yes. Do you remember that property I told you about?" He asked with his beautiful blue eyes lit.

"Yes. The one by the lighthouse?" I asked, trying not to assume.

"Yes. I closed on it yesterday and I have to meet with some contractors tomorrow. If all goes well, I will be gone for about a week or so to help them get everything situated." Well, this conversation definitely took a turn I didn't expect. At least it wouldn't bring forth too much emotion before breakfast, except for the fact that I was sure to miss him while he was gone. But who was I to say anything about that. I was just gone for a week, myself.

"I see." I said. I took a generous sip of my coffee, letting the fusion of the caramel flavor dance on my tongue as I quickly sharpened my intuition for the topic at hand. The expression on my face must have told Jasper that I was spying between the layers of what he was telling me.

"I know the timing really sucks, Angel. You just got back in town and now I might have to leave. I wish it weren't so, but unfortunately it is. I am sorry." He said, with a gleam in his eyes that brought the sincerity to his words I had been seeking with my spiny sense. Without it, I may have second guessed what may have really been going on.

"Don't be sorry. It's okay." I said to reassure him. I didn't want him to feel burdened by our relationship when it came to his own priorities. "Do you need someone to look after Lucas?" I offered. "Or are you planning on taking him with you?" I asked.

"That's very sweet of you to offer, Angel. I was actually planning on taking him with me. There's plenty of space for him to run around on the property." He paused to take a sip of his coffee. "I'll know more after my meeting later on today." He replied.

"Okay, I really need to get downstairs to get ready for work before I'm late. Plus I wanna catch Jamie before she heads out to the gym."

"That's fine. I have to go upstairs to shower and get ready too." Jasper said with another kiss, this time on my lips." *Damn! I never even brushed my teeth!* I laughed to myself, hoping my morning breath wasn't too alarming. Thankfully he was smart enough to keep it a quick peck!

"OK! So I'll be hearing from you this afternoon then?" I asked before downing my own cup of coffee and setting the mug inside the sink to rinse.

"Yes, I'll text you after my meeting." Jasper said as he hopped off the bar stool. I watched as he reached across the island for a bag of dog treats to lure Lucas upstairs with when my eyes caught sight of the opened envelope from the card I gave him. I quickly scooped up my purse before he could make any mention of it and I swear, I couldn't get out of there any faster.

"Sounds good!" I said, nearly running to hit the button for the elevator. "Bye Lucas!"

"Slow down, Silly girl!" Jasper called out. I could hear the discernment in his chuckle when he figured out my reason for running. "Bye, Angel! Hope you have a good day!"

"You too! Good luck with your meeting!" I shouted back from inside the elevator. I could feel my face turning beet red as the doors closed. I don't know why I was so embarrassed about my feelings, but I was. And I knew that he was well aware of them now that he had read my card.

Chapter 37

J amie was sitting on the couch, tying her sneakers when I walked through the door. She looked up at me and smiled.

"Hey you! How was it? Must've been a fun night if you stayed over. Did he like the card you gave him?" Jamie asked with her eyes wide as she eagerly anticipated my response.

The last thing I needed right now was for her to be worried about me. And without any solid evidence to confirm my feelings about last night's dinner aside from Jasper openly acknowledging that something wasn't quite right about Sam and Lena, I didn't want to give her any cause for concern. Even though I was very appreciative over how protective Jamie was over me, I also knew I had to be cautious in what I said to her. I had to think quickly, so I threw her the details about Jasper having to leave town.

"I asked him not to read it in front of me." I replied. Jamie just smiled because she knew me well enough to know why I would say that to him. "He must have read it though, because it was sitting open on the counter this morning.

"Oh yeah? So... What did he say?" She asked.

"He didn't say anything. I left before he had the chance!" I laughed.

"You're so silly." She giggled. "I'm sure he loved everything you wrote! So will he be coming on Friday night?" She asked.

"Oh shoot! I forgot about that!" I pensively replied. "He said he wouldn't miss it when I asked him, but he also told me this morning that he might be leaving town this afternoon. He's going to be staying at the house he just bought for a while to help the contractors get the renovations started. Now, I honestly don't know if he'll be here or not."

"Well, that stinks! I wouldn't write it off just yet, we still have all week. Maybe he'll be back in time." Jamie stood up from the couch and tossed her gym bag over her shoulder. "Well, I gotta go, hon. Keep me posted! And tell Jasper I said congrats on the house!"

"Okay, I will! Have a good day." I said.

"You too!" She called out as she was leaving.

~

I was walking home from work at the coffee shop when I heard my phone ringing from inside my purse. I quickly drew it out, hoping it was Jasper, but it wasn't. The area code was from Wakefield, Virginia. I couldn't imagine who it might be because I honestly had no friends who lived there. And it wasn't AJ's number, so I knew it couldn't be him.

"Hello?" I asked as I answered the call.

"Good afternoon. Miss Taylor?" asked the female caller.

"Yes, this is her." I replied, trying to remember where I'd heard her voice before. A light bulb suddenly went off inside my head and I knew in an instant. *Detective Stacy!*

"This is Detective Stacy calling from the Wakefield Police Department. I'm calling to inform you of the current status of AJ Stratton's case." A storm of emotions cascaded over me and quickly took hold of my breath.

"Miss Taylor, are you there?" She asked.

"Yes, I'm here… I'm listening." I replied, shakily as I tried to collect my nerves.

"AJ is currently being detained until his trial. His court date is set for October 25, 2012. With your signed statement as witness and given the circumstances, it is my duty to keep you informed on all matters of this case. The statement you signed is all that is needed, but you are welcome to testify if you feel called to." I let out a huge sigh of relief. I knew there was no way I would be able to stand up there and relive everything by testifying against him in court. All I really wanted to do was tuck it all away in my past and move on with my life.

"That's great news!" I said. "I really appreciate you giving me a call,

Detective. Thank you."

"As I said previously, it is my duty and also my pleasure to hear that this news puts you at ease. Hope you have a pleasant day." The detective said warmly.

"Likewise." I said, mirroring her professional tone as I pressed the end button on the call.

I sent a group text out to Abby, Mama and Jamie to inform them all about the news I had received from the detective, when I got home. I knew Abby and Jamie were both still in school and wouldn't be able to reply. Mama replied back to me in a private text.

Mama:

That's great news, honey. Thanks for keeping us informed. It's all in God's hands now. I'm sure everything will work out the way it's intended to.

Me:

I hope you're right.

Mama:

Just have a little faith. At least we won't have to worry about him for a little while.

Me:

This is true. Thanks Mama. Love you!

Mama:

You're welcome, Baby. Love you too! (Hugs)

Chapter 38

I welcomed the sound of thunder as my head hit the pillow for my afternoon nap, before work. Listening to the falling rain had always helped me to fall sleep. With the news I had just received from Detective Stacy, my emotions were all over the place.

On one hand, I was relieved that this chapter of my life would finally have some sort of closure. I had hopes that this would bring AJ the wake up call he was needing to truly find his peace and end the suffering I knew he had been internalizing all along.

I hated that our relationship had to come to where we were, but I also realized that some paths lead us to uncharted territory when we made the choice to travel so far in the wrong direction. I was still very angry at him for what he did to Abby. Even with that anger, I still cared about him and where he might end up. I knew I no longer wanted to be with him, it wasn't anything like that. To me, love was like a running faucet, even when you choose to turn it off, the water would still linger somewhere through the pipes. I don't think I could ever stop caring about anyone I had chosen to care about. And AJ was no exclusion from that, despite everything he had put me through.

Knowing I wouldn't have to testify eased any anxiety I had been holding onto in terms of what would happen in court. I couldn't blame myself for being honest. For telling the truth. My truth. If only I had spoken up sooner, I would have saved myself quite a bit of suffering. But that was all water under the bridge now. As long as AJ wasn't a threat to me or Abby, I couldn't really ask for much more than him coming to terms with whatever brought him to the darkness that had consumed him. The rest would be whatever karma he had coming. Justice would be served and I was putting the outcome in God's hands, knowing I did what I had to do in order to keep the cycle from continuing on with someone else.

Then there was this giant puzzle of drama lurking between Jasper and me. Even though I had yet to even come close to solving it, the love between us somehow seemed to overpower everything else. His love for me was undeniable and filled me with hope for a new life. A life with someone who truly honored me in every way. A way I deserved. Just imagining his beautiful face brought me warmth. I held onto that image as I closed my eyes and drifted off to sleep.

~

When I got to work at Silver Linings, there was a card with a single red rose laying across it sitting on top of my desk waiting for me. The card was from Jasper.

Hi Angel,

Thank you for the beautiful card. I'm not sure why you wanted

me to read it alone, but I do want you to know you can always tell me anything. I will never judge you for how you feel. I loved every word you wrote inside that card.

It made me really happy to know that you could feel even close to how strongly I feel about you. I honestly feel like you were sent to me from heaven. A gift from my parents? Who knows? I just know that I felt it the very first time I laid eyes on you and if there is one thing I want you to hold on to while I'm gone, it's knowing that.

I know things seem really messed up right now with everything I have going on, but I promise you, they will get better. All I can do is ask for your patience as I take this time away to gather my thoughts on how to tell you about everything. I know you need to know, Angel. I just need a little time.

I'll call you later tonight when we get settled in.

You have my heart always,

Jasper

~

Jasper kept his promise and called me later that night after I got off the phone with Abby. She was happy to hear the news and again it didn't seem to matter to her nearly as much as it did to me. I was baffled at how insignificant everything seemed to her, but also relieved that she wasn't so affected by it all.

I told Jasper the news I had received earlier that day from Detective Stacy. Just like Mama, he was happy for me and relieved that we wouldn't have to worry about AJ for a while.

Apparently, AJ was on his own as far as legal counsel. Jasper's lawyer had advised him that he wouldn't be able to represent AJ. I completely understood where his lawyer was coming from. It made sense that it would be a conflict of interest. This meant we could finally start building on our own relationship without the distraction of legal matters. Jasper understood how hard it would have been for me if I had been called to face AJ on the stand in court. He fully supported me in my decision and said he would still try to pull some strings and find him decent treatment for his alcoholism.

Jamie and I celebrated like we always did. We ordered Chinese takeout and watched Sleeping with the Enemy.

"Are you sure you don't want to testify?" She asked me with a slurp of her Lo Mein. "I know it won't be easy, but he might get a longer sentence if the jury hears your statement in person." She added after she finished chewing.

"Honestly, I just want it all to be over with. What I want is for AJ to feel whatever he needs to feel to find his way to peace. There's something he's holding on to from his past. I never figured it out, but I know it's there. It's why he drinks so much. The only time he was ever abusive towards me was when he would drink. If he faces whatever lies beneath the surface and stops drinking, I know he can live a good life." I knew it wasn't what she wanted to hear, but it was how I truly felt about AJ.

"You are so much more forgiving than I am." She laughed. "But I get it." She paused for a minute to consider my point of view. "Well, as it stands, he's probably facing 5-10 years for keeping Abby against her will. I just hope he finds the rock bottom you're looking for within that time frame. Since you have a restraining order against him, you will be notified of any changes in his case."

"That's all I could really ask for at this time. I'll just keep praying that he finds the healing he needs to get his life back on track." I said.

We finished our dinner off with a giant bowl of rocky road ice cream and retired for the night when the movie was over.

Chapter 39

Jasper

I was only about 45 minutes away from home, but far enough for me to shut myself out from the world I was in. A world torn between everything I was building with Carla and the power Lena held in her hands to completely destroy everything she and I had built. I knew I couldn't hold onto this much longer before Carla would inevitably find out the truth. I wanted very much to come clean. I also wanted to become a father, but this was not at all the way it was supposed to happen.

The idea of my blood mixing with Lena's chilled me to the bone. I was already feeling horribly guilty about letting Sam down. Hurting Carla in this whole process was something I just couldn't seem to bear. I hated myself for the mess I was in.

I came here for clarity, to find a way to tell her the truth. Instead I buried my head in the sand, distracting myself with the work that needed to be done on the house. I couldn't help myself from imagining a life here with Carla in it. I wanted everything to be perfect for when I would bring her here to see it.

Lena would not stop calling me. Each time I saw her name flash across the screen of my cell phone, I refused to answer. I knew she wanted that money. And I refused to give it to her until I knew for sure that this baby was actually mine. She may have had me by the balls, but I wasn't born yesterday. Something in my gut just told me I wasn't wrong to question whether that baby was mine. Maybe I just didn't want to believe it. Either way, I had to call her out on her bluff. I could only hope she wouldn't do anything stupid before I had my answer.

Each morning, I sent Carla a text to let her know I was thinking about her, but I hadn't actually spoken to her until that Thursday evening when I needed to let her know I wouldn't be able to make it to her birthday celebration. I didn't feel right telling her through a text message. I wanted to be there for her more than anything else in this world, but I still couldn't find a way to tell her the truth.

~

Carla

The week slowly dragged on. I looked forward to Jasper's text each and every morning. The only thing of significance that happened all week was when I felt like I was being followed again on my way to work at the coffee shop on Wednesday morning. I told Brooke about it when I arrived and we went to lunch that afternoon to try and decipher the clues together. Neither of us were able to crack the case.

When Jasper called to tell me he wouldn't be coming to my party, I was so excited to finally hear his voice, but the news he delivered had completely devastated me. His words, "I wouldn't miss it for the world, Angel" rang through my ears all week, and I was really looking forward to seeing him. I honestly thought he would show up. I didn't let on to him how devastated I was when we spoke on the phone because if his hands were truly tied, I didn't want him to feel guilty about not being able to make it.

"Okay, I understand." I said trying my best to reassure him, but my tone had definitely clued him in on what was lying beneath the surface of my words.

"I hope you're not too upset, Angel. I'll make it up to you, I promise." Jasper said.

"I'm not. I'm fine. I completely understand." I said, trying to solidify my previous attempt at making him feel better about the situation.

"Alright, Angel. I hope you have a great time with your friends. I'll talk to you later, Baby. Don't forget, those lips of yours belong to me!" I laughed.

"You don't have to worry about that anymore. I promise. I'll talk to you tomorrow. Good night." I said.

"Good night, Angel." Jasper said before he ended the call.

Chapter 40

Friday morning came and went. I walked through the day in a cloudy haze of disappointment. Everyone would be coming over later that night to celebrate with me and I was in no mood to party. Not without Jasper. Everyone would have their significant others by their side except for me. Even Dillon was coming to be with Jamie. The idea of being the only lonesome wheel at my own birthday celebration was very upsetting to me, despite my attempts at trying to be strong about it.

When I got home from work that evening, I found that Jamie had, in fact, gone all out. Even though I had specifically asked her not to, I wasn't at all surprised that she didn't listen to me. And who was I to fault her? I would have done the same in return if it were her birthday. Apparently, she'd taken the day off from school to tend to all the catering needs and decorations for my party.

I was greeted by a colorful "Happy Birthday" banner, hanging on the outside of our front door. There were black and metallic gold and silver balloons tied up at every corner of the apartment and each place setting on the dining room table had been sprinkled with matching confetti. It was beautiful and festive and I was so grateful to Jamie, I honestly couldn't help but cry when I took in the view.

"It's beautiful, Jamie. You didn't have to do all this!" I said, wiping a tear out of my eye.

"Hey, don't mention it! You should know... I did it because I wanted to, not because I felt like I had to." She replied.

"I know. Thank you. I really appreciate it," I said as I extended my arms to embrace her in a hug. I may not have been in the mood to party, but her generous offer of time and energy in planning everything truly meant a lot to me.

I had no other choice but to go through the motions while Jamie and I got ready. I knew it was important to her that I enjoyed this party, so I put up a front just to let her know how much I appreciated her and all of her effort.

I wore a form-fitted plum red gown with black printed roses strewn across. The fabric was of stretchy cotton and the printed roses were raised in a velvety texture. The dress rested off my shoulders and required a strapless bra to wear underneath. If I hadn't been a c-cup, I could have not worn a bra at all, but I wasn't that daring in my size. I paired the dress with my black, strappy sandals I had scored on our last trip to the second hand store that Jamie and I shopped at. After a gaze into the mirror, even I was impressed by my reflection. I looked stunning, even though I felt so crumby inside.

We greeted everyone that came through the door with a smile and a drink. First to knock was Breana and Ryan. They both looked amazing in their formal wear, as usual. Apparently, Brooke and Jason took the elevator up with Alex and Mandy. We heard them laughing at the fact that they were all headed to the same place when we opened the door.

I got an early start on my wine, hoping it might cheer me up on the inside. I was feeling warm and toasty when they brought out the karaoke machine. A surprise gift to me from Jamie. She knew I always loved karaoke, in spite of my stage fright. She always admired my courage to stand up there and sing my little heart out even though I could barely breathe. Tonight was different though. I just didn't feel like singing. I could play pretend all night, but being able to sing would honestly be too much. Thankfully everyone else partook in the karaoke festivities in good sport and made it a night to remember for sure.

When Brooke stood up to sing "Alone" by Heart, I couldn't help but be reminded of Jasper's absence. Everyone here was in a couple and I was, in fact, *alone*. The song really hit me. Heart was one of my very favorite bands. Alone was one of my favorite songs by them. I quietly slipped out onto the balcony for some fresh air to escape the vulnerability of my emotions. Thankfully, Brooke's astonishing powerhouse of a voice captured everyone's attention enough that no one seemed to notice me leave the party. I was relieved because I really did want them all to enjoy the party, whether I was or not.

I stepped outside to find a warm breeze and a bright night sky. The city lights weren't enough to keep me from seeing the stars. I silently made a wish that Jasper would soon return. Even if he had to miss my party, I felt so much happier when he was here. It wasn't that I couldn't be happy on my own, it was more like I was disappointed because he was gone. I was so wrapped up in my emotions, I barely noticed the music of the party had come to a stop. I took notice when I heard the beginning of the Bon Jovi song begin. What I was really shocked to hear was the voice I heard singing when the lyrics began.

♪I guess this time you're really leaving... I heard your suitcase, say goodbye♪ I had no idea who it was that could sound so much like Jasper's voice. *Was it Ryan?* I think I was missing Jasper so much that I just really wanted to believe it was actually his voice.

♪Well as my broken heart lies bleeding... They say true love, it's suicide♪ Hmm... I wondered. *No, definitely not Ryan. Maybe Alex?*

♪You say you cried a thousand rivers... and now you're swimming for the shore....♪ *No! It couldn't really be him! Can it?* One thing I knew for sure, I was tired of guessing!

I opened the sliding glass door and stepped inside to find Jasper stunning blue eyes staring back at me, singing into the microphone with a voice I had no idea he had inside him. It should be noted, I was probably biased. Hearing his voice was probably the single most beautiful thing I had ever heard in my entire life.

Between his sapphire blue-eyed gaze and that heavenly melodic voice of his, it was difficult for me to draw my attention away from the trance I was under, but I did. One look around the room at all my friends and the smiles on all their faces said it all. A surprise appearance and beautiful serenade of the song "I'll be there for you" by Bon Jovi was epic and everyone in the room felt it! For a second, I wondered if they all knew and had conspired against me. At this point, it didn't even matter to me anymore because I was so happy to see him and that he was here with me.

When the song ended, I ran across the living room to Jasper and wrapped my arms around him so tight, I almost knocked him right into the karaoke machine.

"Hey Baby." He laughed. "Did you miss me?" He asked. I didn't answer him with words. Instead, I pressed my wine stained lips into his so hard, he had no other choice but to kiss me back. And when he did, it was like we were both transported to our own little world. Neither of us with a care in the world that everyone was still staring at us. Our kiss was finally broken when everyone started clapping.

I broke free and gazed into the ocean of his sapphire blue eyes. "You're here! You're really here!" I said, half sobbing into the crook of his neck.

"I wanted to surprise you, Angel. You look beautiful, by the way." Jasper said as he pressed another kiss onto my forehead.

"That you did! I'm so happy you're here!" I cried. By now, I was already on my 3rd glass of wine and my inhibitions had long taken off with the breeze I had felt on the balcony. I had an idea! I walked over to Jamie and whispered in her ear as she was searching for the next song.

"Yes! You should totally do it!" Jamie blurted out so everyone could hear. A moment later, Breana handed me the microphone and the music started. I sang my tipsy little heart out to Jasper while everyone watched in amazement. Crazy for You by Madonna was my song to him because it was exactly how I felt in the moment. My stage fright had found me on a few notes where I had to steady my breath, but the applause I received afterwards had told me I had done well enough.

When my song was over, Jamie called everyone over to the dining room table for cake and presents. Jasper and I shared the first piece and after we finished eating, he pulled me aside to tell me he was going to go upstairs. After working all day on the new house, he truly was tired. He thanked Jamie for the invitation to the party and all her hard work and said goodbye to everyone before he left. He asked me to join him later, after the party was over when I walked him out to the elevator.

"By the way, I have a new pin code. You'll need it to get in. Please make sure you remember it and don't give it out to anyone." He said.

"I would never." I said. I wasn't quite sure why he thought I would give it out in the first place.

"I know you wouldn't, Angel. I just wanted to make sure you knew to keep it private." He said, reassuringly. "I'll see you in a little bit, okay? Promise you won't keep me waiting too long." The hunger in his eyes was far from being lost on me. "Oh, and leave the dress on, please. I want to be the one to take it off you." And just like that, he drew the butterflies to the surface of my belly before disappearing behind the elevator doors. *Tease!*

Chapter 41

━━◦◦◦◦◦━━

Silver Linings: Book 3
Sneak Peek Teaser

My world shattered in an instant. The look on her face was one that could honestly tear my beating heart right out of my chest. I never wanted to hurt her. It was my plan to tell her everything. I knew it was a long shot. I never expected her to understand, but I was hoping that she might. All I really wanted was to see her happy for one weekend before I would ultimately let the chips fall wherever they landed. Being honest was my only fighting chance to keep her. Now, she knew everything. Well, she knew enough, at least, to know I had kept this giant secret from her. And now she felt betrayed. I could see it in her eyes when she looked up at me. The sadness.

How could I be so stupid to let her find out this way? If only I had chosen to man up when she needed me to, I would never be left with the memory of that expression on her face before she took her things and left me. I didn't even have the chance to explain.

Maybe I didn't deserve her in the first place. After all, she was perfect. Why would I think I was even worthy enough to have her as mine? I had absolutely no regard for whether I was worthy or not. I knew I wasn't gonna let her go without a fight, even if it took my last breath! Even if I had to wait, I would be there for her when she was ready. If that time would ever come. At this point, I could only hope it might.

Carla

How a girl could go from being the happiest in the world to being the saddest in a day's time was beyond me. After my party, Jasper and I had spent the night together. When I arrived at his penthouse, he was like the icing to my belated birthday cake. We spent half the night in bed together making love. We were both longing for each other so badly, that our passion for one another had swallowed us up into our own little cocoon of ecstasy.

It was our world. Nothing else existed but the heat of the fire that raged on between us. Little did I know that the following day would bring me news that would not only devastatingly burst that bubble of light we had been surrounded by since we'd met, but also drive a perfect storm of chaos, full of harsh realities that had purposely been sent with a mission to divide us.

Afterword

About the Author

Originally born in Queens, NY, Elisa Ann Pratt currently resides in south Florida with her husband, two teenage sons and three fur babies. She deals cards for a living by night, while pursuing her passion for writing during the day.

Her talent was first noticed by friends and family when she began writing poetry as a little girl. In middle school, one of her poems won a contest, landing a spot in the school newspaper.

In high school, she took several creative writing courses and wrote poetry and short stories for fun, mostly entertaining her friends, but also utilized her writing as an outlet for her most inner thoughts. She always knew she was a writer, life just seemed to get in the way, as it does for many.

Elisa has always been a hard worker, taking pride in the various hats she wore as a young adult where she sometimes worked three jobs to make ends meet.

On social media, you'll find she loves to cook, listen to music, take photos and read books. She truly believes we are all gifted with our own unique talent to share with the world and goes out of her way to support anyone with courage to chase their own dreams and aspirations.

Elisa finally feels she is in the right place to showcase her writing to a greater audience where she hopes to relate to, entertain and inspire others.

Stay tuned for Book 3 in the Silver Linings Series
   Follow me for updates at: Linktr.ee/elisaannpratt

Also by Elisa Ann Pratt

Being a published author is my dream come true. I want to express my deepest gratitude to my readers for being the greatest part of my writing journey. Without you all, none of this is possible.

I have met some amazing people in my Indie Author journey who have found such a special place in my heart. Your support, guidance and love has made this process a deeply enriching experience. I truly love you all from the bottom of my heart.

P.S. If you or someone you know is struggling with domestic abuse, please know there are resources available that can help you.

National Domestic Abuse Hot Line

Available 24/7

English and Spanish and 200+ other languages with interpretation services

phone: 800-799-7233

SMS: Text START to 88788

Add image

Silver Linings: Drawn
  (Book 1 of the Silver Linings Trilogy)